WITCH WAY DID HE GO?

WITCHLESS IN SEATTLE BOOK 8

DAKOTA CASSIDY

DAKOTA CASSIDY

Witch Way Did He Go?

Published 2018 by Dakota Cassidy

ISBN: 9781790894369

Copyright © 2018, Dakota Cassidy

❀ Created with Vellum

ACKNOWLEDGMENTS

Cover artist: Renee George

Editor: Kelli Collins

My darling readers,

Please note, the Witchless in Seattle series is truly best read in order, to understand the full backstory and history of each character as they develop with every connecting book.

Especially in the case of the mystery surrounding Winterbottom (I know it drives some of you crazy. Sorrysorrysorry!). However, his story is ever evolving and will contain some mini-cliffhangers from book to book. But I promise not to make you wait too long until I answer each set of questions I dredge up.

And, too, I promise the central mystery featured in each addition to the series will always be wrapped up with a big bow by book's end!

Also, please note, I'm prone to taking artistic license with locations and such, so forgive any places near and dear to your heart if they're not completely accurate.

This will be the last addition to the Witchless series

for 2018, so from all the gang (and me, too) in Eb Falls, here's to a wonderful holiday season filled with love, laughter, family, and friends!

See you in 2019 with more titles, like *Witches Get Stitches* and *Witch Lash*, in the *Witchless in Seattle Mysteries*!

Dakota XXOO

WITCH WAY DID HE GO?

*M*y friends, this is probably the most difficult account of my time with Win (or maybe in my entire life) that I'll ever relay to you. Let me just begin by saying that day, and the awful, horrible, terrible days after everything fell apart, began like any other.

Well, almost any other day.

We don't plan an enormous Thanksgiving feast at Mayhem Manor for half of Eb Falls every day, but the arguing over my deader-than-dead palate and Win's refined, snobbish one were par for the course.

That was just like any other day or week or even year. We always playfully argued over my crude twelve-year-old's taste buds. I like Twinkies and Cheese Doodles—so sue me.

But how it all ended? That was definitely not like any other day we'd had—*ever*. Not in all the time we'd known one another.

Because it ended with me begging Baba Yaga to help me find Win. Me, begging my nemesis—the woman who'd banned me from my coven for life—to use whatever connection, whatever magic spell she had up her sleeve, good or bad, in order to help me find out where, *why*, Win had quite abruptly disappeared.

And I'm here to tell you, there was a lot of ugly crying, a lot of scraping, a lot of laying my guts, naked and vulnerable, out on a metaphoric table for her to pick through at her leisure like a starving vulture.

I'm also here to tell you, I don't care how that sounds or how it looked or that I lost every shred of pride I ever possessed in the begging.

I did it, and I'd do it again. I'd do it a million times over if it led me to Win and his safety. Desperation didn't even begin to describe my state of being, but I can tell you, this was the biggest mystery I'd ever solve.

Anyway, begin at the beginning, right? Like I said, we were in the throes of prepping for a Thanksgiving Day feast fit for a king—or at least that's how *Win* planned a dinner party, as though some sophisticated, worldly king were coming to dine with us here in Eb Falls.

Which is a lovely touch, don't get me wrong. I'm sure as a guest, arriving to neatly dressed waiters and waitresses holding luscious delights like shrimp-wrapped bacon and mini-quiches is far more appealing than being greeted by me with a plastic platter of peanut butter and jelly rollups on flour tortillas.

But it was nothing if it wasn't a production where

Win was concerned, and probably, if truth be told, one of the things I truly loved about him. I don't like admitting it, but there you have it.

He's detail-oriented, and he knows how to make everything perfect, from the moistest, plumpest turkey, golden brown and roasted to juicy heaven (sorry, Strike!), right down to the little triangular fold he'd insisted upon at the beginning of the roll of guest bathroom toilet paper.

I tried to tell him no one would even notice how the TP was folded, but he said it was a subliminal element meant to add to the feeling of being pampered via a pile on. When you added up all the small-ish details, they became one big treat you remembered fondly, and they made you feel important and well loved.

Still again, I tried to remind him we were talking Sandwich here—a guy who, on a bet way back in middle school, had eaten a pickle and sardine hoagie with mayo. I honestly didn't think he was even going to notice where the toilet paper *was*, let alone that the ends were folded in a triangular shape. But Win said everyone deserves to be treated like royalty, even men who eat sardine/pickle and mayo sandwiches.

Then I figured I'd better pick my battles with Win, or I'd end up eating caviar (fish eggs—ick) and foie gras (goose liver—double ick). That's a big *gak* from me, thank you very much.

So yes, he was being a stickler for the details and driving me straight up a wall, but if I'd known…

Wait. Isn't that what everyone says? *If I'd only*

known, I would have [fill in the blank]. Don't we all say that after the passing of a loved one or when something horrible happens? *If only...*

Argh! It's woefully cliché, and trite in the saying.

But dear Heaven above, it's *true*. It's the truest truth there is.

You'd think, dealing with the dead as often as I do, I'd have paid better attention to the notion you should never leave things—important things—unsaid. Yet, *my* things, the things I've wanted to say to Win for a very long time, aren't things I can say without consequence —without making him feel worse than he already does about not being here on Earth with us…with me.

Still, had I known I might never hear him call me "my dove" again, I'd have said them anyway. I'd have summoned the courage, risked our deep friendship, risked it all just to say them—and damn the consequence.

Because in the end, when you might never again see the one person who brought life to your colorless, witchless world, who made you belly laugh, who told you stories, who gave you purpose again, who made you secretly smile to yourself, who treated you as though you were made of fine porcelain yet wrapped in steel, you'll wish you had.

You'll wish it with every agonizing breath you take.

And I do. *I wish.* I wish with every cell in my body— every inch of my existence.

As long as I live, I'll never forget the last conversation we had. I can barely manage to remember what I had for dinner yesterday, but I can remember our final conversation word for word...

"*No Cheez Whiz?*" I asked the ceiling, with a squeal of fake clutch-my-pearls outrage. Logically, I knew my ghostly Spy Guy didn't linger up there in all his ghostliness, but I couldn't break the habit of looking upward at the sound of his voice. "C'mon, Win!"

"Stephania, only a Philistine would serve Cheez Whiz on crackers to their guests as a prelude to their Thanksgiving feast. It's almost as unseemly as your weenies in a blanket. Thus, why do you even bother to test my patience this way when you know good and well what the answer will be?"

I dropped my phone, where I'd been typing in the never-ending list of items we needed for our big Thanksgiving Day bash, onto the table.

Everyone was coming. Dana, Sandwich, Enzo and Carmella...even Melba, who couldn't get time off to go back east to be with her family. And Win wouldn't be satisfied until he'd driven me crazy with the smallest of details.

"How would you even know what's served at a Thanksgiving feast, Mr. Snooty-McSnoot? You don't celebrate Thanksgiving in the UK."

"Ah, 'tis true," he drawled, his voice rich and resonant in my ears. "But I do know how to entertain,

5

Stephania, and one does not do such with canned cheese and ranch-flavored crisps."

I popped one of those ranch-flavored crisps in my mouth and made a face. "There's nothing wrong with a Cool Ranch Dorito. It makes a perfectly good appetizer."

"For a Philistine."

Belfry giggled, rolling across the kitchen table as we sat by the bank of windows and watched the wind howl and bend the bare trees in our backyard. "You're so chi-chi-foo-foo, Winterbutt," he teased in his tiny squeak.

"*Dah*, Zero. You are, as little winged-man say, chi-chi-foo-foo. If we very lucky, in Russia, we have bread *with* butter for fancy-schmancy occasions. Why you make such fuss?"

"Well, old friend, we're neither in Russia nor serving Cheez Whiz, and that is my final answer."

I chuckled at his disagreeable tone. Win always became grumpy when we teased him about his penchant for turning everything into an event literally fit for the queen.

I sighed and shivered when I looked out the window at the pouring rain, watching the trees and the last of their leaves scatter in the wind. It was chilly enough to hunker down with sweaters and scarves now, my favorite kind of weather.

"Touchy-touchy." I held up a hand. "Fine. No Cheez Whiz. Now, what was it you said about the lettuce? Radicchio or no radicchio? Which, by the way, is just plain silly. Lettuce is lettuce, Spy Guy. It's green and crunchy and you slather it in dressing to hide the green taste."

I think I heard him almost gasp his British indignation, but he stifled it and said dryly, "Radicchio is not lettuce. It's a *chicory* and green does not have a taste, Stephania."

"Then explain green Jell-O."

He rasped an exasperated sigh, indicating I'd gone too far. "Stephania, must you be so contrary?"

I giggled and reached for my cup of coffee, taking a sip and smiling. I loved this time of night. We were all home, warm and safe after a long day at Madam Zoltar's, reorganizing the store while we had downtime during this, one of our quieter months.

We'd eaten our dinner, Whiskey was at my feet, and Strike cooed from his corner of the room, where he snoozed on his heated bed.

This was the time we spent chatting or playing a board game (believe it or not, Win and Arkady use Belfry as their earthly assist and both play a strategically mean game of Monopoly, which shouldn't surprise me. They *are* dead spies), or simply watching TV.

After the last murder we'd solved together, life had been mostly quiet, especially since our new friends, Trixie and Coop, had moved on to Cobbler Cove, Oregon. In fact, we often joked they'd taken all the murderers with them, because they'd been involved in two since leaving, and we hadn't even had a minor mystery to solve.

Well, aside from the mystery of the tattooed hand Win claims to have seen the night he was killed, which remains a mystery, and not one I don't poke around in when I'm by myself—because I do. I still have absolutely nothing to go on, but I haven't forgotten about that tattoo, believe you me.

Anyway, for the time being, we'd decided to let sleeping dogs lie and enjoy life. Our summer had been filled with helping folks cross over, and chatting via Skype to advise Trixie and Coop from time to time when they needed help with a crime they were investigating.

We'd also spent many weekends barbecuing with Dana and Melba, now officially a couple, Enzo and Carmella, Chester, and Sandwich, who had a new lady love named Katrina. We'd even done a little bit of boating, and I took my first very rough attempt at fishing.

As the season ended and the tourists left, naturally business slowed, and we began to focus on fall activities like Halloween and Thanksgiving.

All was right in our worlds, and I, despite Win's haranguing me about the perfect Thanksgiving dinner, had found genuine happiness in this little niche in life we'd created.

"My dove?"

I sighed, letting my shoulders sag and pouting up at the ceiling. "Sorry. Got lost in my thoughts. What was the question?"

Belfry flew around the ceiling, his tiny wings fluttering and making Whiskey bark. I hushed Whiskey with a hand to the top of his head, scratching his ears to soothe him.

"Winterbutt asked why you had to be so contrary," he chirped like the parrot he was.

I rolled my eyes and rose from the table to hunt down a Ring Ding in the cabinet by the coffeepot. "Oh, right. I'm the one being contrary because no one is going to care what kind of lettuce we have. Sandwich probably can't even pronounce radicchio."

"Stephania! Shame on you. Our Sandwich has come a long way under the watchful tutelage of the lovely Katrina. He hardly ever uses his thumb to bulldoze his vegetables anymore. He's becoming quite the refined gentleman, if I do say so."

I giggled, digging out my Ring Ding from the package and unwrapping it from its foil. "I really like her. She's so lovely and warm, isn't she?"

"*Dah*, my marshmallow-covered candied yam," Arkady agreed with his hearty chuckle. "She has pretty laugh, and she makes Sandwich turn red when he look at her and she isn't watching. Young love is a beautiful thing."

Katrina Waters owned a nonprofit dog rescue. Sandwich, who'd been looking for a canine companion, happened upon her rescue by Melba's suggestion and, as they say in the movies, it had been love at first sight.

At least for Sandwich. For Katrina, it had taken a little more time—like three months' time of many dates, during which Sandwich had put his best foot forward.

Still, they were adorable together. Big ol' Sandwich and teeny-tiny slip of a thing Katrina, who could wrestle a pit bull into submission, were a sight for sore eyes with all their canoodling and cooing.

Not to mention, she loved animals as much as we did—how could you go wrong with an animal lover?

"She *is* lovely, Stephania. I'm thrilled for Sardine and his new ladylove. Now, back to our planning. Where were we?"

Ugh. "Stop picking on Sandwich. And lettuce. We were in lettuce and the ridiculous amount of different varieties. Please, Win, I beg of you, don't make me suffer another second of this. I'll get whatever kind of lettuce you want. I'll fly it in from the Land Where They Make Lettuce. Nay, I'll buy a lettuce factory if you'll just give me one night of peace from this list. I feel like we've been working on it for a hundred years."

"A lettuce factory?" Belfry squealed as he soared across the kitchen before landing on my shoulder, where he couldn't stop giggling.

"A hundred years? Isn't that a little melodramatic? Besides, Stephania, we only have a few days until Thanksgiving. We must prepare. We must—"

"Plan!" I interjected, taking a big bite of my Ring Ding and heading to the fridge to pour a glass of milk. "I know. Believe me, I know. I feel like we're planning to heist Fort Knox, for cripes sake. It's dinner, Win. Not life or death."

"Speaking of Fort Knox," he drawled, winding up to tell me some story or another, I'm sure.

I held up my hand with the Ring Ding still in it as I grabbed the milk. "Wait. Don't tell me. You, on a super-spy mission, in a super-secret land, with a super-secret gadget, foiled a super-bad guy at Fort Knox, right?" I teased on a giggle, pushing the rest of my Ring Ding in my mouth and grabbing a glass.

There was a pause, and then he said, quite dryly, I might add, "No. I was going to say they have a lovely tour at Fort Knox—spies sanctioned by MI6 only, of course. It's not open for mere mortals like yourself. And how can one foil a super-secret bad guy in a super-secret land if Fort Knox is in Kentucky and not a secret at all, Stephania?"

"Ahahahahaha!" Belfry laughed. "He's got ya there, Stevie!"

Arkady laughed his deep gurgling laugh, too. "Oh, my lovely daffodil. You make every day so wonderful."

Pulling my sweater tighter around me, I took a gulp of my milk and shoved the carton back in the fridge. "You men! You're all such men!"

"Indeed," Win agreed on a chuckle. "Now, can we carry on and stop dillydallying? We have a feast to plan, and while I know you don't enjoy the strategy of it all, you'll thank me when you don't have to lift a lovely finger, Dove. So enough of your tomfoolery. Let us complete this eve's task at hand."

I went and sat back at the table and waited for him to finish, dropping my chin into my hand as, once more, I scrolled my list of grocery items the caterers weren't handling like the salads and crudités.

Clearing my throat, I drummed my fingers on the table and looked up. "Win? We left off on radicchio. What's next?"

I was greeted with nothing but the sound of Arkady's light snoring. He must have nodded off from sheer boredom. And seriously, who could blame him? If I loved anything less than actually shopping for the food, it was writing the list for the food we needed to buy.

Now I became annoyed. With a frown, I called, "Win? Hello up there? Weren't you the one who said we had to get 'er done? Let's get 'er done."

I cocked an ear and waited, but still there was nothing but the sound of Arkady's light snoring and Whiskey's heavy breathing as he slept.

Pushing myself away from the table, I clicked my phone off and tucked my hands into the sweater Carmella had so lovingly knitted for me as I made my way out of the kitchen and toward the living room.

Just before I crossed the threshold into the entry-way, I gave him one last chance. "All right, Grudgy, this is your last opportunity to speak now or forever hold your peace."

Pausing by the table against the side of our spiral staircase, I dusted off a fake leaf in the large fall arrangement and waited again. "Crispin Alistair Winterbottom, stop being a curmudgeon. I was only joking. You can have your radicchio, okay?"

Whiskey moaned as he trailed behind me, his big paws padding on the hardwood.

"Wow," Belfry commented on a chirp as he took off again, circling the high ceiling of the entryway. "Sir Crankypants is on the warpath tonight, huh?"

"I was just teasing him, for pity's sake," I mumbled as I wandered into the living room and plopped down on our sofa.

Belfry landed on my shoulder, burrowing into my hair. "And it's not like he can't appreciate a good joke. He's always crackin' with the wise. Maybe he's got some kind of ghostly affliction and it's giving him bad tummy?"

Clicking on the TV, I scrolled our DVR for one of my favorite shows. "He doesn't get bad tummy, Belfry. Ghosts don't get bad anything. He's just being a chump." I looked up at the ceiling. "Hear that, Win? You're being a little childish. No. You're being *a lot* childish, but you let me know when you're done, and if I've had my fill catching up on *90 Day Fiancé*, maybe—*maybe*—I'll consider finishing our grocery list."

I muted the television and listened again, but still nothing.

Dang. Not even a peep.

"Okay, but you're going to regret not telling me what type of potatoes you want when T-Day comes and we only have the kind Philistines use."

Belfry chuckled, but that was the only sound in the room save for the roaring fire Enzo had built for me, because he knew how much I loved coming home to one.

Fine then, I decided as I pulled the soft throw over my legs and hunkered down on the couch to catch up on some of my shows.

But not before I stuck my tongue out at the ceiling.

Take that, Fancy Pants McGee!

CHAPTER 2

"*My malutka?*" I heard Arkady whisper in my ear, his Russian accent pronounced by his closeness.

My eyes popped open, and I caught a glimpse of the old antique clock on the buffet by the fireplace Win had talked me into buying when we'd gone antiquing in Seattle one day.

I squinted. It was four in the morning. Arkady never, ever awakened me. Never. Not once. And Win had only roused me once himself.

Reaching out a hand, I felt around and realized I wasn't in my bed but still on the couch.

Shoot. I hated falling asleep on the couch then having to haul myself up that long flight of stairs to my bedroom. Also, I had a serious crick in my neck and drool at the corner of my mouth.

"*Malutka!*"

"What?" I almost yelled, stirring Whiskey, who still lay at my feet. "What's going on, Arkady?"

"You must rise, now, *malutka!*" he insisted with such urgency, it was as though he'd actually used a hand to shake me.

I yawned and stretched, rolling my head on my neck to ease the kinks. "What's wrong, Arkady? What's so important?"

Looking back now, I realize I should have been far more alarmed that he'd woken me than I actually was.

"It's Zero, Stevie."

"Oh no," I chastised with a shake of my finger and another yawn. "I'm not finishing his grocery list now. No way, Jose. He was behaving like a two-year-old tonight by stomping off in the middle of our conversation. He'll just have to wait until tomorrow because—"

"*Stephania!*"

I clamped my mouth shut and looked at the dying embers of the fire, my head cocked in confusion.

Okay, that was two nevers in one night. Arkady never woke me in the middle of the night, and he never called me *Stephania.* That was reserved for Win and Win alone.

So what the heck?

I slid to the end of the couch and reached down to run my hand over Whiskey's head, letting him know it was time for bed. "What, Arkady? What's going on?"

"I can't find Zero anywhere, my *malutka.* He is…" He paused, then inhaled as though it were a chore to form the words. "He is gone!"

I made a face. "He's not gone. He's probably off flirting with the ladies on Plane Limbo's version of Tinder. In fact, I'll bet his finger's sore from swiping right so much."

Did that sound a little jealous? Petty? I try not to let that seep into my conversations with Arkady or Belfry, but every once in a while, I still felt those pangs about Win and his ex, Miranda, and my insecurities take over.

I have no right to be jealous. It isn't as though Win's professed his undying love to me or we're a couple, but the kind of love Win had once felt for Miranda was something to be envied, even if I didn't have feelings for him at all.

But in honor of our friendship, and due to my deep respect for Win, I kept my inner demons to myself.

"Bah, *malutka!*" Arkady admonished. "There is no swipe anything here, and Zero would not swipe even if he could. You *must* listen to me, he is gone, I say!"

I pushed my feet into my slippers and cuddled Belfry, who'd wormed his way into the pocket of my sweater. Patting Whiskey on the head to indicate this time it was really time for bed, I made my way to the stairs.

"*Malutka?*"

I gripped the banister and headed toward bed. "He's not gone. He's just off doing Win things, Arkady. He does that all the time, doesn't he?"

It was my understanding that Win roamed freely all over Plane Limbo, and there were plenty of activities to attend. I didn't understand the uproar or the tone of voice Arkady was using—so urgent and almost fearful.

"This is what I try and tell you, *malutka*. He does *not* do these things all the time. He *never* does these things. He is always here with me. Right next to me on our bench."

"You have a bench?"

I'm not sure why that was so important to me, but I rather liked knowing they had a place to sit.

"Yes, right by the waterfall. But is that really important right now, kumquat?" he growled in my ear.

"By a waterfall? That sounds lovely."

I reached the top of the stairs and stopped, admiring the long settee covered in embroidered silk pillows we'd placed beneath the bank of windows overlooking our backyard. The moon, high in the sky and no longer covered by clouds, shone through the squeaky-clean windows, glazing the soft eggshell fabric with a soft glow.

"*Malutka!*" Arkady all but shouted, his panic evident. "Why will you not listen to me?"

I flapped a hand and padded down the hall to the most amazing bedroom ever. There were days I couldn't believe how lucky I was to have such a gorgeous place to lay my head.

"I *am* listening, Arkady, and I don't think you need to worry. But tell me this. Does he have to stay near you all the time? Is that some Plane Limbo law? Or does he simply *choose* to stay near you?"

Right here, right at this juncture of our conversation, I should have paid closer attention. For all intents and purposes, Win and Arkady are tethered to me. In essence, they go where I go.

They can mute a conversation out of respect for my privacy. They can roam Plane Limbo quite freely, but they can't stray very far on the earthly plane without me. It's one of the downfalls we joke about all the time when it comes to solving a crime.

If only they could leave my side and see what a suspect is up to when no one is looking or even call for help when I'm in a pickle, I probably wouldn't have as many scars as I do.

I guess I'd never asked if they were also tethered to each other. Still, the whole idea of being tethered should have raised some red flags for me, but I was too stuck on the idea that Win was messing with me.

Arkady huffed as I pulled back the covers of my warm comforter and hopped into my bed, the most beautiful bed, built into the wall, with bookshelves above my head and sitting under a round window.

"You do not understand. I will explain. No, he does not have to stay with me. Yes, he chooses to, but this is not like Zero! He does not wander off this way. I have looked all over Plane Limbo for him. I have asked everyone where could he be? No one knows. I cannot find him, *malutka*! Why will you not trust me when I tell you this is cause for alarm?"

I patted the bed so Whiskey would hop up next to me. I loved stroking his soft fur as I fell asleep. "Of course I trust you, Arkady. I'd trust you with my life. I just feel like Win's making a point, and I'm okay with that. I was teasing him overmuch about this Thanksgiving Day thing. So he's in a huff right now, but he'll snap out of it."

"Aha! But have you ever known Zero to go off in, as you say, huff over something so silly? *Nyet*! He never does this. He is tough as screws. Why would he make with the mad about a salad? That should be first clue something has happened."

Okay, that did make me pause. It was true. Win could take a joke...but maybe I'd been teasing him all this time and he'd been putting on a good face? Maybe I'd finally managed to worm my way under his skin, and this was his way of telling me he couldn't take another second of my Philistine-esque ways?

So I brushed off the notion as I hunkered down under my delightful comforter and told Alexa to turn off the lights.

"It's nails. He's tough as nails. And I think I finally got to him, Arkady. You know how that goes, right? Sometimes you go along for the ride until you can't grit your teeth anymore and then you explode. I bet that's what happened. It's not like we haven't argued over a meal before. Remember our end-of-the-summer barbecue, when he insisted the lemonade had to be hand-squeezed by a Dutch virgin from the Himalayan Mountains or some such nonsense?"

I giggled at the memory as I ran my hand over Whiskey's ears.

"Oh, he did not, *malutka*. The Himalayas are not

Dutch. And he say we should not serve *frozen* lemonade to valued guests."

My eyes began to close and I yawned again. "Yeah, yeah. Do you also remember how many lemons it took to make one stinkin' glass, and the hissy fit of all hissy fits he pitched when he realized I'd snuck in some concentrated lemonade?"

Arkady sighed a raspy, irritated sigh. "Now, now. You did tell story to him, Stevie. You pretend you spend all morning squeezing lemons when really you busy getting legs waxed."

Even as sleepy as I was, I managed to bark a laugh, tucking my hand under my chin. "Yeah, I did, didn't I? And I still don't regret it. What I'm saying here is, Win's very particular, and I love that about him... mostly. I really do, but this Thanksgiving dinner and my pointing and laughing could have been his last straw."

"What does dinner have to do with straw? I do not understand Americans and their strange speak."

"Meaning, he finally became fed up enough to need a break from all my teasing. Ooor you guys are messing with my head."

Now that was a possibility, too. Maybe they were pranking me?

"Why I mess with head? I do not understand this mess with head," Arkady balked.

Uh-huh. "It just means you guys are maybe playing a joke on me to teach me a lesson?"

"Bah! This is no joke, my cinnamon bun. No joke."

Hmmm. I still wasn't sure that was true. Regardless, I conceded because I needed some sleep.

"Listen, if this isn't some joke you two hatched up—and I'm not convinced it isn't—I promise you, I'll apologize to him tomorrow over breakfast, okay? I'll even eat a healthy breakfast that doesn't consist of some form of cake in a foil wrapper."

Arkady huffed again, long and drawn out. "Maybe you are right, but I will tell you now, as the mother country is my witness, I do *not* like. I do not like this at all. Remember Arkady say this tomorrow when you eat healthy breakfast and Win is still nowhere to be found."

Sighing with pleasure in my cocoon of warmth, I nodded and murmured, "I'll remember. I promise, Arkady. Now grab another nap or something and Win'll be back before you know it."

And then I closed my eyes and drifted off to sleep, warm and a tiny bit remorseful I'd made Win stomp off in a ghostly fit of temper.

But I really intended to apologize tomorrow.

Swear.

~

*A*s I dabbed on a smidge of perfume and grabbed one of my favorite scarves, a vintage Hermes in rust and gold, I smiled into the mirror as I caught a glimpse of the day outside.

The wind had died down since last night, and a muted sun was peeking through the clouds, a rarity for this time of year in Eb Falls. The fall colors outside my bathroom window, situated just above my claw-foot tub, were fading as the leaves fell from the trees, but there was still enough to leave me invigorated by the crisp tones.

I tickled Belfry's belly, making the leaf of the large elephant ear plant he snoozed on shift. "Hey, you awake, lover? You don't think I'm going to the grocery store all alone, do you, buddy? I imagine once we're done making this infamous list, we'll need two shopping carts. I need support. So up and at 'em."

Bel stretched his tiny wings, letting them fan out before he yawned wide. "You think Win's over his pout?"

I ran a brush through my hair, tucking it behind my ears, letting the soft curls fall to the top of my collarbones before I straightened the buttons on my purple faux-silk blouse and tucked the front of it into my jeans.

"So you heard the conversation I had with Arkady?"

"Yep," he said on another yawn. "Enough to know Win's a little bent out of shape. Though, it's not really like him to storm off. In fact, it's pretty weird, but we all have our limits, I suppose."

I grabbed a pair of small stud earrings from my jewelry box and put them on. "Yeah. It's not like him at all, but maybe he just hit a wall. Either way, I'll make it right. So, c'mon. Get up and let's grab some breakfast before we tackle the grocery store. We need sustenance to survive what I'm sure is the first of many trips into town."

Belfry chuckled as I left him to his morning routine and headed downstairs to feed Whiskey and Strike before eating that healthy breakfast I'd promised Arkady I'd have in Win's honor.

As I entered the kitchen, the sun pushing its way through the overcast day, painting a beautiful orange and gold glow over the table, I paused for only a moment as I waited for Win to greet me before I went to the pantry to fill Whiskey's bowl and grab some seed for Strike.

When I'd finished the task of feeding the animals and silence still rang throughout the kitchen, I gave in with a smile.

"Okay, Spy Guy. You win. Joke's over. I was wrong to tease you about Thanksgiving dinner. Your eye for detail is, bar none, masterful, and I bow to you, sensei. I apologize for teasing you about how nitpicky you can be. Now, can we cut this out and finish this T-Day list? I do have other things I want to do today, like finish watching *90 Day Fiancé*. I fell asleep in the middle of it, and I won't be able to think straight until I know what happened to Nicole and Azan in Morocco."

Pausing, I cocked my head and leaned on the island, running my hands over the smooth, cold marble. "Wiiin. C'mon. Come out, come out wherever you are, or I'm going to have Twinkies and Swedish Fish for breakfast!"

Nothing. Still absolutely nothing. Cupping my chin in my hands, I sighed.

"*Malutka*," Arkady called out, somber and husky.

I grinned and stood up straight at the sound of Arkady's voice. Well, at least someone was awake up there. "Yes, my borscht-loving Russian Angel?"

"Win is still not here on bench. Did Arkady not tell you last night this would happen?"

CHAPTER 3

I heard his anxious tone, and took note of it before dismissing it entirely again.

But hell's bells, right at that moment, I should have listened to Arkady. I'm pretty stubborn, I'll give you that, and I really felt like Win was playing me, but I'm not so stubborn I don't usually pay heed when someone who's not prone to histrionics, like my dead Russian spy, is all but panicking.

Though, in my defense, at this point I was still convinced this was a joke they'd cooked up together on Plane Limbo, laughing like a couple of fourth-graders at how funny it would be to teach Stevie a lesson for being such a sass-mouth.

So, I decided I could play along. "So he's still angry, I gather?" I asked, the smile still on my face as I picked up Whiskey's bowl, clean as a whistle after finishing his breakfast, and grabbed Strike to give him a quick cuddle.

"This is what I try to say to you!" he huffed in an explosion of words, as though he'd been holding them in. "I do not know *what* he is, my *malutka*. I do not know if he is angry. I have not seen him since last night. It is as I told you, he disappeared as I napped and has not returned to our bench since. We always watch the sunrise by the waterfall while we wait for you to awaken. *Every single day*. We have never missed one time. Something is wrong. Something is terribly wrong!"

Now, more than ever, I really thought they were in cahoots. Did Arkady really expect me to believe Win had disappeared into thin air when he'd never disappeared for this long before? And this bit about Arkady napping? As I recall, Win said they didn't sleep up there. Come now. After all they'd taught me? I wasn't buying it. I felt like I was being pranked.

Except, you heard Arkady snoring, Stevie. You've heard him snore before. Yes, yes. But I ignored this very important clue and stayed with the idea they were having a go at me.

Strike rubbed his cheek against mine before I set him back on the floor and grabbed my purse, throwing my phone inside with a sigh. I pulled my chunky gold sweater from the back of the kitchen chair and rolled up the sleeves.

"So question, Arkady?"

"Yes, *malutka*?"

"How could you have been *napping*," I made air quotes with my fingers, "if you guys don't sleep? I distinctly remember Win saying something to that effect. Have I caught you in a fib, my favorite Russian?" I teased.

"Do you not hear me snore?

"Bah! It is Zero who does not sleep, and because we are silly men and we like to compete, I pretend Arkady stay awake as long as him. I close my eyes when he isn't looking."

As crazy as that sounded, I believed him. They did like to one up each other with stories of their spy days. "Of course you'd turn it into a competition. Whatever was I thinking?" I asked on a chuckle.

"This is why I tell you something is wrong, zucchini bread!" he insisted, really playing up the urgency in his tone.

"Hmmm. I don't think anything's wrong, Arkady." I wanted to follow that up with the words *and you know it*, but I was going to let them have their fun for the moment.

Belfry buzzed down through the hallway, his tiny body the color of a marshmallow, pulsing through the air until he landed on the kitchen island, where I tied the tiniest scarf ever made (A Barbie scarf, if you must know, but don't tell Belfry) around his neck to keep him warm.

"Man, Winterbutt's not fekkin' around, huh? I tried calling him while I was upstairs, but I got the old silent treatment. You think he's okay, Stevie?"

I scratched under his chin and wondered it all the

men in my life were pranking me—even my loyal familiar.

Nah. Bel wouldn't do that. Right? They'd all male-bonded, without a doubt, but Bel's loyalty would always lie with me, even though technically, he wasn't really my familiar anymore because I was no longer a witch.

"Not you, too? Of course I think he's okay, Bel. He's just making a point. It's not like him to make a point for this long, but that's what he's doing." I looked up at the ceiling. "Isn't that right, International Man of Mystery? And Arkady's helping you make your *point*, isn't he?"

When I was once more greeted with silence, I nodded with a smile and jabbed my finger in the air.

"See? Making a point. Either way, I guess the grocery store can wait another day. I have to make a run to Madam Zoltar's, anyhow. I left some papers there we need to file away."

"Stevie? You are going to simply ignore Arkady's concern?" he asked, irritation simmering beneath the surface of his words, almost shocking me until I caught myself and remembered he was once a spy, too.

They gave good face, and I'm telling you, that's exactly what I thought he was doing. Playing a part—and playing it well, I might add. Which explains why he was so revered in the spy world, I suppose.

Yanking my keys from my purse, I jingled them. "Weeell, I'm not exactly ignoring it, my friend. I'm just putting it off for the moment. I have a zillion things to do and I don't have time for another one of Win's teachable moments right now. We have guests coming, and I have things to accomplish before then. So let's revisit this tonight, okay?"

I was only saying that because I knew it would soothe Arkady. I didn't think we'd have to revisit anything. I truly, truly believed Win would be back, in rare snooty/snarky British form by then. I swear I did.

Arkady grunted in response, which was perfectly fine. He had a part to play, and he was doing it justice.

"So are you coming? Or do you need to catch up on some sleep, Brad Pitt?"

"Who is this Brad Pitt?"

I rolled my eyes as I made my way to our stained-glass front door. "An actor. One you're giving a run for his money. Never mind. Are you coming with or not?"

"I will come with you, but I am not doing so without great reluctance!"

"Yeah, yeah," I teased, pushing the front door open. "Come, my reluctant Russian, let us make with the haste!"

Bel buzzed his way to my shoulder, and that's when I felt him lean in, pressing his small snout to my ear. "Hey, you really think they're pranking you?"

I chuckled as I stepped onto the front porch, chock-full of mums in every available color and baskets filled with every variety of pumpkin sold in Eb Falls (Win loved to fill the coffers of the local farmers). I inhaled the chilly air and smiled before hopping down our wide front steps. "I do."

"I hear you, little insect!" Arkady called out, making me stop as I beeped the car door open.

Wow. We were really doing some method acting here, huh? "Now, that's not nice, Arkady. You're taking this a little too far. Please apologize to Belfry."

"Humph," Bel snorted, dripping sarcasm. "I don't need his apology. He can suck it."

I chucked my familiar under the chin before getting in the car. "Two wrongs, buddy. You know the score. No return fire, please."

Arkady grated out a sigh, one that whizzed through my ears. "I am sorry. That was rude. I do not mean to be rude, but you will not listen and I am frustrated."

I turned the heat on and situated myself in the seat before turning on my Pandora playlist to one of our recent favorite Broadway soundtracks, *Wicked*. The song "For Good," one of Win's favorites (and mine, too), secretly made me think of him.

"Thank you, Arkady. Now both of you hush. Kristin Chenoweth and Idina Menzel are calling my name." As I adjusted the rearview mirror, I asked, "You hear that, Win? I'm going to sing my face off to your very favorite song from *Wicked*—*loudly*—until you show yourself!"

When I was greeted with yet more deafening silence from the afterlife, I did just that, using my touch screen to bring up the song.

And as we zipped along the beach road toward town, I sang the words at the top of my lungs, "*Because I knew you—because I knew yooou, I have been changed for gooood!*"

~

"There's my girl!" Chester called out just as I was leaving Forrest's café, Strange Brew, armed with a cup of coffee and a bran muffin.

Not my favorite muffin by a long shot, but I hoped Win was looking down and smiling at my healthier choice while he gave me the silent treatment.

I swung around on the sidewalk to face him, smiling at his sweater vest with a turkey embroidered on the pocket. Chester was everything you'd order up if orders for a grandfather were for the taking, and I loved everything about him, from the tip of his shiny shoes to the top of the tuft of white hair he had left on his head.

"Well, hello, handsome!" I said with a wink, dropping a kiss on his cheek. "What are you up to today?"

I had to laugh at how close Chester and I had grown, considering when we'd first met, he'd sort of accused me of murder. Also, I loved that he didn't hold any grudges where Forrest and I were concerned. We hadn't worked out, but we'd remained cordial friends, and Chester was fine with that.

As he smiled at me, his warm grin a ray of sunshine under what was quickly becoming an overcast day, he tugged a lock of my hair and squeezed my cold hand with his warm one.

"I'm up to no good as usual. What are you up to, young lady?"

Rolling my eyes, I sighed. "Errands. So boring. But

now I'm headed to Madam Z's. You want to come with and we can catch up? I feel like I haven't seen you in forever."

"It's only been a week, but I can't today, pretty lady. I'm keepin' an eye out on the café for the kid, but save me some time later this week, and we'll have a sit down and gab a couple of hours to chew the fat."

"You, sir, are on." I dropped another quick peck on his round cheek before heading down the sidewalk toward Madam Z's just as it began to lightly sprinkle.

We didn't keep regular hours like we did in the spring and summer months, and were mostly by appointment only in the fall and winter, but Liza still manned the register for us when she wasn't in grad school, and we still loved her just as much as we always had.

I was looking forward to seeing her for Thanksgiving dinner, where all her youthful exuberance for life and her studies would keep us smiling for days after she went back to school.

I typed the code for the alarm on the door and pushed it open, closing my eyes and relishing the stronger scents of sage and lavender from the candles we sold.

There were days I still couldn't believe how lucky (and honored) I was to have taken Madam Zoltar's place. Even though I could no longer communicate with anyone but Win and Arkady (the how and why still remained a mystery to us all), stepping into her shoes had given me purpose again.

And part of that was due to Win's insistence and his ghostly guidance with our clients, something I also considered myself insanely lucky to have.

I chuckled to myself. Maybe Win's teachable moment was working?

Popping my eyes open, I stepped inside, prepared to handle some minor paperwork and straightening of the postcard rack while I waited for Win to finish out whatever this was he was doing so we could get our shopping done.

At least, that was the plan—until I opened my eyes and saw the condition of the store.

It literally made me gasp out loud.

"What the fluff?" I muttered, just as I heard Bel's feet skitter their way to the top of my purse, where he perched on the edge.

"Sweet pickled relish, what the heck happened?" he squealed, pushing off to take flight.

Had we been robbed?

As I took in the smashed candles and the overturned smudge sticks, I almost couldn't breathe. What...?

Papers from my desk caught my eye—scattered from one end of the store to the other, and a room away, mind you.

The register, something we cleared out every time we closed the store, was literally cracked in half, the two pieces lying on the glass countertop—which also had enormous fissures in it.

All the essential oils—hand-mixed by a local artisan,

and once lined neatly on a shelf—were smashed to smithereens, the liquid seeping over the hard floor and filling the air with myriad scents.

Even the neon Madam Zoltar sign, which I hadn't noticed when I'd unlocked the door, was broken, chunks of the sharp pieces of plastic littering the floor.

I found myself speechless.

Who would do such a thing? We didn't keep much in the way of value in the store, other than the random items we sold from local shops, but then, did burglars really think about those things when they broke into a place of business, looking for booty?

"Malutka?"

I blinked as I began picking my way to the back room, where the beaded curtain separating our reading room from the store had virtually been torn from the doorframe, leaving the beads sprinkled everywhere.

My hands instantly went to my temples, a headache forming as I took in our reading table, broken to bits, the candleholders that had once sat in the middle, tossed to the side of the room.

"Arkady?"

"What...?" He cleared his throat, his question full of wonder. "What happened?"

I blinked again, my purse sliding off my shoulder and dropping to the ground. "I...I don't know. Who would do this? *Why* would someone do this?"

"It is mess, my pickled cucumber. A terrible, horrible mess. You must call police, and remember, do not touch anything!" he warned.

Instantly, I threw my hands in the air to avoid cont-amination. Arkady was right. I needed to call Dana and Melba—maybe even Detective Meaniebutt (who still held a ridiculous grudge about losing his partner after I'd found out the man was a murderer. Such an incon-venience, right?), and report this.

Yet, the moment I thought to kneel down and grab my purse, was the moment a disembodied voice boomed into the room as though shot from a cannon.

"Save him!" it yelled, so loud, so fierce, I found myself stunned by the intensity of the echo it left behind. The two words swept around the room in wind tunnel fashion.

My eyes went wide, instantly gazing at the ceiling, which had begun to shift and quake. I'm not sure why I always looked to the heavens when a ghost made contact. I've never been able to actually see them except for once or twice with Win. In my mind, they hovered over a room just like they did on television.

Anyway, things began to get very dicey then. Surprise, quickly followed by panic, set in as I watched the ceiling above me ripple and the voice bellow once more. *"Save him! Save! Save! Save!"*

What in all of heaven was happening? How could I hear this voice when I'd only been able to hear Win and Arkady for all this time? What did this mean?

"Saaave hiiim!" it shrieked with rage, making the entire store quake and rumble. *"Listen! Listen! Liiiiisten!"*

"Save *who?*" I cried when, from out of absolutely

nowhere, an arctic blast of wind began to blow, tearing at my skin, clawing at my face.

Ice began to form on the walls, thick sheets, growing, spreading across the room, climbing upward as the wind howled and tore at my clothes, pulling at the buttons of my shirt.

"Belfry!" I screamed, tiny crystals of ice clinging to my lashes while random objects and paper swirled about my head, dancing and bobbing. *"Belfry, where are you?"*

"Malutka, put your head down! Push toward the wind! You must get to the door!" Arkady cried, his voice filled with fear.

Fear. Something I'd never heard so clearly from him as I did now. There had been times when I'd battled with a bad guy, and I could detect a smidge of concern in his tone, but he was almost always as levelheaded as Win.

Yet, not now—not in this moment. Now, he was yelling panicked directions at me, his voice almost drowned out by the roar of whoever was screeching.

"Malutka, Belfry, take cover!" Arkady hollered just as a chunk of the ceiling fell on the floor, narrowly missing me—because I'm nothing if I'm not good at taking direction—as I dove for the corner of the room.

As the sheetrock fell, crashing to the floor, ice and water flying everywhere, the voice picked up momentum. *"Save him! Save him! Save the imposter!"*

The imposter?

Bel buzzed to my shoulder, burrowing into my hair. "What the feck is going on, Stevie!?"

Turning, I pressed my back to the wall and inched my way upward seconds before a river of water gushed across the store's floor. Bone-chilling and dirty, it began to rise, creeping up so quickly, I thought we'd have to snorkel our way out.

"*Malutka*, you must run! Run for the door! Get out! Get out now!"

And I did just that.

Okay, I didn't run. I paddled, or maybe waded was a better word, but while I headed for the door, the voice —and I'm assuming he's the one responsible—began hurling things at me, clunking me in the head with a heavy candle.

My hand flew to my head, rubbing at the spot as I tried to push through the water, my clothes becoming so heavy I had to yank my sweater off. Dang it, that hurt!

Now, I wasn't so much panicked as I was angry. In all this time since I'd been witchless, I'd forgotten how to deal with a variety of ghosts because I let Win do the dealing for me. He was always my go-between.

But no more. Today, Stevie Cartwright was going to take back the reins, for a little while at least. All of the old maneuvers I'd once used when dealing with a malevolent force came back to me at once, but the one lesson I'd learned first was to never let a ghost take control.

With water pouring down on my head in buckets,

with icy fingers, soaking wet clothes and a cute pair of shoes totally ruined, I stopped mid-escape and yelled, "Hey, up there! I can't save anyone if you take me out! Knock it the heck off, you unruly beast, or I'm going to banish you to Plane Eleven!"

And then everything went silent.

Blissfully, eerily silent, giving me a moment to gather myself enough to realize something huge had just happened.

But what? And why?

Almost waist-deep in water, I looked around the store—a place I loved nearly as much as I loved our house—and let out a small whimper, forgetting about the enormity of what had just gone down.

It was a disaster. The store was a complete wreck. We'd be here for days cleaning up.

Realizing I was out of breath, I looked up at the ceiling. "That's better. Now, what in all of the realm was that about and *who* is the imposter?" I asked as, without warning, the water began to magically drain away.

But there was no answer, which appeared to be the standard response from the afterlife today.

"Popsicle?"

"Yes?" I answered, my teeth chattering as I watched some of our store items float past me.

"What is this Plane Eleven?"

I almost laughed. It was a threat I'd used often when I was a witch, but truth be told, I'd never done it before. "It's a plane for very bad people. Obviously not one our loud friend wants to visit, judging by the way he quite suddenly stopped creating havoc." Shivering, I looked around for my purse as my thoughts raced, but I needed some answers here. "Arkady, is anyone with you? Can you see who did this? Usually Win has a handle on what's going on up there."

Arkady, riddled with panic moments ago, scoffed derisively at me. "*Dah, malutka.* You do not say?"

All right. This joke had gone too far now, and I was tired of playing along. "Okay, my hunky cosmonaut, you guys have had your laugh. I already told you, I get it, and I went too far teasing Win. Now where is my spiteful little British spy? We'll need a big dose of the afterlife's help for this one, methinks."

"*Stephania,*" he rasped, his tone so heavy, I was glad it wasn't sitting on my shoulders. "I will say one more time. Win is *gone.* He is gone, and I don't know where he is. I repeat. *Zero. Is. Gone.*"

CHAPTER 4

*T*his is the part where everything goes a little sideways, spirals downward, and then goes a lot topsy-turvy. This is the part where I finally take Arkady seriously.

A chill so violent, so dark and black, rolled upward from my toes to the top of my head, and I began to shake, almost unable to catch my breath from the trembling.

This is the part where I realize a piece of me has suddenly gone missing, and I'm terrified because I don't understand the reason why or, most of all, *how*.

Still, I straightened and forced myself to approach Win's disappearance like I would any other mystery. With logic and critical thinking.

"Okay. I get it," I whispered and paused, lost in a swirl of racing thoughts.

I looked up at the ceiling, fighting the tightness

growing in my chest and the sick feeling in my stomach. There was no need to panic yet. Not yet.

Clearing my throat, I slogged my way toward the last place I'd seen my purse as everything around me began to shift once more, and the water, miraculously, all but dried up. Then the ice on the walls began to shrivel, and the freezing-cold temperatures rose.

I think at this point my mouth fell open. I hadn't experienced paranormal activity on this level without Win in quite some time, and it took a moment before I began to feel less fearful and instead sought to understand the purpose behind the event.

Whatever that warning was about, whomever it was from, it would have to wait for the time being. Win was missing—and nothing else took priority.

"*Malutka*," Arkady said, with a snap-out-of-it tone.

Gathering my thoughts, I looked upward. "Yes, Arkady?"

"You are okey-doke, my biscuit?"

Swallowing hard, I nodded as I discovered my sodden purse, still at the doorway to the back room. Oddly, the moment I picked it up, it went from a sloshy mess to dry as a bone, and seconds later, my clothes followed suit.

This was so odd…

I'm not sure what kind of voodoo was going on here, but whoever that ghost had been—and again, this is an assumption on my part; I don't know if it was a ghost or maybe even a demon—it was pretty powerful.

"*Malutka*, answer me," Arkady prodded with a

forceful tone.

"I'm mostly okay, if not chilled to the bone and stunned. Forget about my condition. Let's attack Win's disappearance the way we do any other crime scene. The way Win would want us to go about solving his disappearance. Tell me the last thing you remember seeing before Win disappeared. Was he there on the bench with you before you nodded off?"

"*Dah*, and he say you are Philistine because you like the Cheez Whiz. He sit right here with me on bench. We sit together every day, delicate butterfly. *Always*."

"But you never go anywhere else? Like maybe bingo or a club or…I mean, I don't know. Are there such things on Plane Limbo?"

It was just a big, vast canvass of nothing in my mind's eye. Sure, I occasionally thought of a waterfall because Win had mentioned one once when we'd crossed over, of all things, a pig. But I never gave it much detail or depth. Now I wondered if there weren't places to go. Like grocery stores and malls…

Oooo, were there malls in the afterlife?

Sorry. Got sidetracked there.

"Plane Limbo is what you wish it to be, *malutka*. It is different thing to different people. For us, it is peace and quiet on the bench by the waterfall, watching as the souls come and go."

That made sense. Win and Arkady's lives had been full of intrigue and mystery, with more chaos than the inside of a vacuum. Peace and quiet was likely something they'd both crave.

Running a hand over my currently drying-at-the-speed-of-light hair, I frowned. "And you've asked your fellow Plane Limbo friends if they've seen him?" I asked as I made my way to the reading room—where the table was put back together as though it had never been broken in a bunch of pieces, making me frown.

"Of course I ask, Stevie. I ask everyone all night. But you know how it is here. Some people are not reliable due to bad experience. The, how you say…trauma?"

Ah, yes. Trauma. Sometimes, if a soul is taken harshly from this world and they end up on Plane Limbo due to unfinished earthly business or doubt about crossing over, they can present as very confused.

But if not even a confused soul had mentioned Win's whereabouts, that was cause for concern.

But wait a minute. I froze in place, not only because an idea crossed my mind—but because now, every single thing that had been torn asunder, broken, knocked over, was mending itself right before my very eyes.

"Stevie," Belfry whispered in hushed awe, "I've never…"

My mouth fell open. This was like watching someone wave a magic wand and make everything right again, and believe you me, I'd seen that happen a time or two.

"Sweet Kremlin," Arkady breathed followed by a whistle. "How can this be real, my butternut squash? Did you see this before they take your witch powers?"

I inhaled while I watched the cash register rebuild

itself while I stared on, aghast. Listen, I'm a witch, and I've seen lots of spells cast in my time. I've seen all manner of amazing events, but never with this sort of magnitude.

"No," I said on a breath out. "I've never seen something this big. I don't understand…"

But as I said that, I realized I was becoming sidetracked by the bibbidi-bobbidi-boo of it all and not focusing on the problem at hand. We were losing time and becoming distracted from the real problem. My spine stiffened. "Arkady, we need to focus. We can't deal with the reason this is happening right now. We need to find Win first."

He cleared his throat with a gruff cough. "*Dah*. Yes. We must stay focused. So where were we?"

Tucking my purse over my shoulder, my eyes still wide with wonder, I answered, "You said you asked around on Plane Limbo about whether anyone had seen Win."

"*Dah*. No one has seen Zero. I check three times today. I ask about tall, handsome man with sharp suit and blue eyes."

My heart clenched hard at Arkady's description of Win, and that's when I thought of something else. Something that made me gulp hard, but the question had to be asked.

"Okay, so here's another question for you. Have you seen the light recently?"

"To the Great Beyond, *malutka?* Is this what you ask?"

Holding my breath, I could only nod as I decided to make my way back to the front of the store.

Arkady must have realized what I was really asking, because he quite suddenly hissed an answer. "You do not think, Stevie...? No! He would never! I do not believe! Zero would never leave you!"

Fighting the tears forming in my eyes, I gripped the repaired counter, staring at the postcard rack next to the restored glass surface. "Are you sure?" I squeaked, forcing myself to say the words that needed saying, but also because I needed to air them out—put them out into the universe. "Maybe he finally decided to cross, Arkady. Some souls waffle for a very long time, and then a feeling or a particular calling overwhelms them and they make a snap decision. It happens all the time."

My chest constricted as though someone had tightened a corset around my torso, but I was once a medium. I knew what happened when the right time came for a soul to pass.

Yet, he gasped in clear outrage. "Zero would not leave!" he thundered, totally catching me off guard with the fury I heard in his voice.

Arkady was always so lighthearted and easygoing, but his loyalty to Win shone through every word he spoke.

Bel burrowed deeper into my neck. "I gotta agree with the crazy spy upstairs, Stevie. Win would never leave you—us. *Never*. And even if that was a choice he decided to make, don't you think he'd at least say goodbye first? Would he up and leave without looking back? C'mon, Stevie. I know you know better."

I inhaled again, a shuddering breath as I closed my eyes and regained my composure. "You know what the calling's like, Bel. It's irresistible to most."

"Yeah. I know what's it's like, and Win's not *most*," Belfry retorted, sounding a little angry with me himself. "So how 'bout you drop that nuttybutter notion right now and move along with another theory, Cowpoke? Because that one sucks stinky rotten eggs."

I held up my hands in surrender, swallowing my threatening tears. "Okay, okay. It was just a theory. Win would want us to consider every angle."

And he would. He'd tell me to think logically rather than emotionally. I didn't doubt that for a second. I didn't like it because this wasn't some nondescript case where I didn't know the victim. This was Win. My Win. *Our Win.*

Bel took flight from my shoulder and buzzed around the store before he landed on the windowsill under our Madam Zoltar sign. "Yeah, but he wouldn't want you to consider *that* angle. So next theory, please, Sherlock."

Biting the inside of my cheek to keep from crying, I still secretly wondered if that wasn't exactly what had happened to Win. How did one up and disappear from a place he'd never once left unless they did so by choice? Where else could he have gone but to another plane? As far as I knew, it was very difficult to plane hop.

Though, that thought made me cock my head and ask out loud, " Arkady? Have the two of you ever plane hopped? Could Win maybe have gone off to another plane?"

"*Malutka*," Arkady said on an aggravated sigh. "You know how difficult this is to do. You say so yourself many times. *Nyet*. We never plane jump unless you count airplane. This we do often."

Still, I clung to the theory because it was, at the very least, a theory. "But Win was a spy, Arkady. It's not like he isn't used to difficult missions, right? Or you either, for that matter. In fact, I'd bet he'd consider it a challenge. And plane hopping isn't impossible, it's just hard."

"Do you use noggin today or did you lend to someone else? He left in middle of conversation with you, *dah*? If Zero decide to plane hop, which is crazy, he would not do so while he talk to you. He has fancy manners. That would be rude. You know this about our Zero. Plus, he would never leave *you*. Find new theory."

Okay, he had a point. Win likely wouldn't disappear in the middle of a conversation, and that only made me worry more. I sort of didn't give a lot of credence to the part where Arkady pointed out Win would never leave me, his manners aside.

Maybe because I wasn't thinking about our personal relationship? I was thinking of us as a whole —all the working parts.

Trying not to let him or Bel see I was shaking, I leaned against the counter and pretended to approach this with a level head. "Fair enough. So, Arkady, do you have a theory? Any theory at all?"

There was a long pause, a drawn-out silence as Arkady considered, and I prayed with everything I had he'd have some ideas...until he said, "*Nyet, malutka.*"

His tone was so full of remorse, my pulse began to slosh in my ears.

My mouth went bone dry and my knees went weak, but I managed to hang on. "Then give me a minute to think, because I'm not sure where to go from here."

I began to pace, because movement felt like the only answer to this cagey fear crippling my limbs, somehow still marveling at the event that had just taken place.

As I looked around, I couldn't believe just moments ago it looked as though a tornado had whizzed through Madam Z's, and now, everything was right back where it had been when I'd left yesterday.

Yesterday...

Before Win had disappeared. This was crazy. He'd never done anything like this before, and just as Arkady said, he would never leave a conversation the way he'd left ours last one. I didn't know where to go from here? How did you investigate a mystery in the afterlife?

I had to wrap an arm around my middle to keep from losing my morning coffee. Win wouldn't want me to give in to my fear. He'd want me to figure out what happened to him—someway—somehow. It's how we'd met. It's how we'd bonded. It was the glue that held us together, among other things, and I refused to believe we wouldn't continue to solve mysteries.

We were a team, with sidekicks and everything. Win would never willingly walk away from us.

Which could only mean he'd been taken unwillingly?

Maybe by a spiteful warlock named Adam Westfield?

My stomach plummeted, and I had to bend at the waist to keep from losing what little was in my belly.

It had been a long, long time since I'd given Adam Westfield my valuable time and thoughts, but the very idea of his involvement, of any kind, petrified me.

"What're ya thinkin', Stevie B?" Bel asked as I came to stand at the picture window and gaze out at the rain splattering against the sidewalk.

I watched as the food trucks, very much alive with patronage, even in the rain, doled out goodies to the people of Eb Falls. I watched as everyone went on about their day and, for a split second, I envied that.

There'd always been a fear, somewhere deep inside my brain, that Win would either choose to cross over or Adam would exact revenge on me through him.

The former being the reason I've never told him how deep my feelings for him are—because I never wanted him to feel any manner of guilt if he ever chose to leave Plane Limbo. How could I tie him to this world —to *me* that way?

But if Adam was involved…

"Stevie?" Bel called me once more.

I licked my lips, forcing the words from my mouth as though they were pushing their way through peanut butter. "I'm thinking Adam Westfield. What if he has something to do with this?"

I know Bel tried to hide his gasp, but he was unsuccessful. "You don't think…"

"I don't know," was all I could manage to say as the world tipped sideways for a moment before righting itself. Even breathing his name was like a punch to the gut.

"This is bad warlock, yes, *malutka*? The bad man who take your witch powers?"

"Yes. Yes, he's the one who took my powers, and he's tussled with Win before. Have you heard his name mentioned at all, Arkady? Surely, someone as powerful as Adam would come up in conversation?"

"*Nyet*," he replied tersely. "No one speak of him but Win. He tell me all about what he do to you."

I breathed a semi sigh of relief as my cold chills evaporated. At least there was that to comfort me. I couldn't bear it if Win was hurt because of me, and trust me, Adam would steal Win's soul if there was a way, just because he was so close to me and Adam knew it would leave me in devastation.

Squaring my shoulders, I gave a sharp nod, and maybe I dismissed Adam too quickly, but there was no reason at this point to suspect he was responsible for any foul play. Besides, I couldn't linger on the subject of the spiteful warlock for too long or I'd crumble from terror.

"Okay then, back to the drawing board."

As I said the words, I looked down at the floor under the window…and frowned.

How had that postcard gotten there?

I looked back at the rack, and every single one of the postcards that had been scattered throughout the store were now back in place, exactly as we'd left them last night.

Bending at the knee, I grabbed it and held it up to the gloomy light from outside, my fingers clammy.

"*Malutka?*"

"Spring," I murmured. "This is a postcard inviting people to visit Eb Falls in the spring, with a picture of the sheet music from Vivaldi's concerto for…spring. It's Win's favorite of *The Four Seasons*."

"What does this mean, cupcake? Explain to Arkady, please."

My heart began to throb and my pulse pounded in my ears as I gripped the postcard. "Win always said spring was a time for *rebirth*. Oh, Arkady, you don't think…" I stopped speaking as my mind reeled and my stomach lurched yet again.

"What, Stevie?" Bel squawked, buzzing around my head, his wings flapping with a fury.

"I…I think he's done what he always said he'd do if the opportunity ever presented itself."

"What he will do?" Arkady asked, his voice tight and strained.

"A body," I answered after a dry gulp. "I think he's trying to possess a body."

CHAPTER 5

"This is, as you say, bananapants, *malutka*! You do not believe Win is looking for body to inhabit, do you?"

We'd all piled into the car and headed home in almost complete silence, none of us able to articulate words after I'd suggested Win was body hunting.

Now, as we sat at the kitchen table, the afternoon ahead of us, I pinched the bridge of my nose. "I don't know what to think, Arkady! I mean every postcard in the whole stinkin' place was right back where it started, all neatly returned to their holders but that one. The sheet music for Vivaldi's spring concerto—Win's favorite of the four. Can you explain that?"

"Zero like lots of different music, Stevie. Except your Back Alley Boys. He does not like them. He say they sound like kitty-cat dipped in acid."

I almost chuckled, until I remembered I might

never hear Win complain about my love of the Backstreet Boys again if we couldn't find him.

"It's Backstreet Boys, and hello. I reiterate, Win loved Vivaldi's spring concerto because it represents *rebirth*. He's said so himself several times. Get it? Rebirth? Sounds like a huge clue to me. Also, do you recall seeing any other postcards with his favorite music on them left out of the mix like that, in an obvious place, rather than being put back where they belong the way the rest were? If that clue had teeth, it would have bitten us, Arkady."

"Bah!" Arkady growled a deep rumble of noise. "This is dangerous, the body jumping! Zero would not risk his soul like this. If he do this, he could lose his soul. His *soul*. He was always smart spy, Stevie. That is stupid, stupid move. Win is not stupid."

I gnawed on the inside of my cheek before I said, "But does the risk outweigh the reward, Arkady? Getting his life back? Being able to enjoy all the fruits of his labor, like this amazing house and all that money here on this plane? Eating caviar and that disgusting spreadable liver pate that looks like something Whiskey would eat? I think I know Win well enough to know he'd say no. The risk doesn't outweigh the reward because the reward is huge!"

I yelped the words as my excitement over having a lead grew, making Whiskey bark sharply at my feet.

Belfry hopped off the table and landed on Whiskey's back, latching on to his ear and soothing him. "It's okay, boy. The crazy lady's just cookin' up some crazy. I won't let her infect you. I got you."

Dropping my palm on the table, I balked. "I am *not* crazy, Bel. Think about it. He's talked about it more than once. You know he has. Somehow, someway, Win found a way to send us a message, and that message was he's body hunting. Or maybe…maybe he's already found a body. I don't know…I don't know how he did it, but he's done it before. You know he has."

Oh, my stomach was in some uproar, I'll tell you what. If Win was doing this—if he was trying to possess a body, what body was he hopping into like he was skipping from puddle to puddle, and where? Where was the body? It could be anywhere in the world. How had he even found a body that matched all the strict guidelines he had—that matched what I'd once jokingly called his life code?

The code where he wouldn't possess a body that had any relatives or anyone who could identify him ever—the code where he'd never do it if it would cause anyone even a second's pain.

He had so many rules of ethics, he'd never do something haphazardly. I knew Win almost as well as I knew myself, and the body he took possession of would have to be a near perfect match to all the rules he'd made for taking over someone's life.

"*Dah, malutka*, he has done this before but he cannot sustain body snatching. You have seen this, too. It never last."

Hopping up from the table, I shook a finger at the

ceiling. "But I've also seen Adam Westfield do it, Arkady, and he *was* able to sustain it for a long period of time—days, in fact. Who knows how long he could have sustained it if I hadn't intervened?"

"But bad man is warlock, *malutka!* Zero is different. He is dead *human*. Not the same," Arkady protested with vehemence.

I squinted at the ceiling, my feet like ice. "But he's talked about it with you, hasn't he, Arkady? Don't bother to lie to me either because I know the two of you are thicker than thieves. He's talked about the idea on more than one occasion, hasn't he?"

I listened to Arkady's uneven breathing, and that was all it took for me to know what I said was true.

"Yes. Yes, he has spoken of this with me, and I have begged him not to do it because I do not wish to lose my dear friend if he make mistake. I cannot think about him losing soul. I will not!"

Oh, if he succeeded, I was going to kill him myself! "I knew it! And I have a feeling that's what he's doing right now. I feel it in my gut, guys. The problem is, he's never possessed a body when we weren't there to help him in case something happened. When I wasn't there to help guide him back if necessary."

Fear streaked through my heart. Dear heaven, so many horrible things could happen. So many...

"You can fix if he breaks his soul, *malutka?*"

I almost laughed at Arkady's description but the cold sweat breaking out on my forehead reminded me, this was anything but funny. "I can't fix it, no. But I think I could still tell, even without my witch powers, just from the body's language if the attempt was failing."

"Okay, so where, Stevie? Where is Win performing this invasion of the body snatchers?" Bel asked, worry riddling his voice, because he knew.

Bel knew all the things that could go wrong with something as dangerous as possessing a body.

With a racing heart, I clenched my fists. "I don't know, but if I know Win, he's left us clues. He's planned. He's prepared. He's strategized."

"And he say nothing to Arkady," my Russian spy muttered, the hurt in his voice ringing loud and clear. "He make plan to do crazy stunt and he do not share with his friend."

When I gazed up at the ceiling, it was with sympathy. Arkady loved Win. They'd become the greatest of friends in the afterlife, even though they'd been archenemies while they'd been alive.

"You know Win, Arkady. He would never do anything to intentionally hurt you. Never. I'm betting he didn't tell you because the opportunity arose quite suddenly."

Arkady clucked his tongue, the clicks sharp in my ears. "I do not think so, *malutka*. He would not tell me because he knows I would try to talk him out of the crazy. Zero is smart man, but he know Arkady well. He could not accept his fate. I can. We disagree, as all great friends do from time to time. Still, it hurts my heart that he do not trust."

If Arkady was here, I'd give him a big hug to ease his sadness. "I don't think it has to do with trust. He trusts you implicitly, Arkady. It has to do with not letting you talk some sense into him. Sometimes, when you don't want to know the truth, you turn a blind eye, and the truth is, possession is very, very dangerous, and he knows it because I've told him as much. Which is also why he probably didn't let *me* in on this little stunt, either. I'd have put the kibosh on it so fast, his British head would have spun."

"But we still do not know for certain it is possession," he said stubbornly. "Until we know for certain, I will not go into, as you say, hissy. I will wait."

"Then what else could it be?" I asked as I rose to make some coffee. I needed caffeine if I was going to think straight. Caffeine and something in my stomach.

A well-nourished spy is a strong spy, Stephania. Your mind and body must be equal in wit and strength. Win had said that a hundred times if he'd said it once. So I grabbed a Pop-Tart while I was at it.

Now that we had a workable theory, I felt less terrified. I didn't love running around in the dark with no particular path in front of me. But at least if we considered possession, we had a purpose, and we could branch out from there.

Turning to face the room, I raised an eyebrow. "So, guys? Any other theories? Because if you got 'em, I'm open. Otherwise, we go with possession."

There was a lot of grumbling and shuffling around

up there as well as in the kitchen by Bel, but no one openly disagreed with me.

I took a bite of my chocolate-filled Pop-Tart and grabbed the carafe for the coffeepot. "Then possession it is for two-hundred, Alex!"

~

"*Malutka*, your eyes, they falling."

Yes. Indeed. My eyes were falling. They were falling because I'd been at this for almost ten straight hours with nary anything but a potty break and some water, and I still didn't know what to do next.

I popped upright at the sound of Arkady's voice and blinked hard, pinching my cheeks to keep my eyes open.

"They're not falling. I'm just resting them," I joked, my voice, even to my own ears, strained and weary.

"You do this for too long. You must rest, my spicy sausage. A sleepy spy is a vulnerable spy."

Massaging the base of my neck, I sighed, cracking my knuckles before planting my finger back on the trackpad and began going through the death notifications within a five-hundred-mile radius one more time.

"I'm not being a spy right now, Arkady. We're not in imminent danger. I don't have to be alert in that way. We're just looking at all the deaths and life-threatening accidents that have occurred within the last couple of days."

Boy, were we. Have I mentioned in the course of just two days—forty-eight hours—there'd been a whole lot of visits from the grim reaper? Car accidents, murder, death by food poisoning, heart attacks, strangulation, drug overdose, and even one death by erotic asphyxiation were just a few of the things I'd encountered as I searched every possible death involving a candidate for a body in which my International Man of Mystery could land.

And it was like looking for a needle in a haystack. I was pretty sure I knew what the minimal requirements Win had for possession were, but the finer details were a little fuzzy. We'd never really discussed them because I'd always poo-pooed the idea.

Pushing the laptop away, I let my head rest in the cradle of my arms for a moment, a throbbing headache slicing its way across my temples.

"We need more information, Arkady. I mean, what if he doesn't mind coming back as a woman? Do we know if that was one of his rules?"

I can't tell you how disappointed I would be if he actually managed that. I'd miss his whiskey-dipped voice, his British accent even if he landed in another male body. But somehow, him calling me "dove" in a woman's voice just wouldn't be the same. Though I'd still keep right on secretly adoring the person he is on the inside. Nothing can ever change that.

Maybe, if he returned as a woman, we could shop together, lunch, braid each other's hair…

I shook my head. Ugh. I was overthinking now.

Arkady began to laugh, that deep chuckle that usually made me smile. "I think not, *malutka.* If our Zero is actually doing this thing you are thinking, the snatching of bodies, he will not come back as anything other than man. Trust Arkady."

My sigh was ragged and full of frustration. "Did he tell you that? Or are you just assuming it's what he'd do? We can't assume anything at this point. I mean, if he's willing to inhabit a woman's body, or even a child's, for that matter, it changes the criteria of my search entirely."

"I will forgive your ears when they not listen to Arkady because you are tired. I will let Winterbottom explain to you himself why he would not come back as anything other than man. But if I know much, I know he would not come back any other way. You must trust me when I say I speak the truth."

I clenched a fist, tight with tension. "Okay, okay. And you're right. I'm being persnickety because I'm tired and I have nothing in the way of leads but this one. This has to be what's happened to him, Arkady. If I don't cling to this theory—this idea he's trying to inhabit a host body—I have nothing other than…"

I couldn't say it again. I wouldn't say it again.

"Other than your bad guy thoughts. Do not think on those, *malutka.* There is nothing to suggest bad man has Zero."

I made a face at the ceiling and rubbed my eyes. "If I listen to you, there's nothing to suggest he's possessing a body. Yet, you still have no other theories, either."

"Stevie? You need some sleep. You're becoming surly, young lady, and my experience when you're tired is you say things you don't necessarily mean," Bel reminded me.

Always my compass, Bel knew me almost better than I knew myself. I hung my head in shame, using the heel of my hand to rub my grainy eyes. "You're right, Bel. I'm sorry, Arkady. This is just so personal... It's not like the rest of the cases we've solved. I'm emotionally invested and it's too hard to compartmentalize. I know Win would have a cow if he could hear me, but I can't seem to help it. Also, I can't stop worrying about..."

I was afraid to say it out loud. Much like the notion that Win had crossed or that Adam had him in his clutches, this almost worried me more.

Bel buzzed to my shoulder and nudged my ear. "Stop worrying about what, Stevie."

"All the things that can go wrong in a possession. What if he's successful and he doesn't..." I gripped my cold mug of coffee until my knuckles turned white as tears stung my eyes.

"Remember us?" Bel finished because he knew I couldn't.

"*Remember us?*" Arkady scoffed in disbelief. "Why would Zero forget? We are his friends. His family."

Sighing, I clenched my fists and stared out at the

dark, choppy waters of the Sound, carefully weighing my words. But there was no way to sugarcoat this kind of information.

"Sometimes, when a spirit possesses another body, signals become crossed and the memories from the spirit's old life get lost in the new host. From what I understand, it can be very frustrating and, in some cases, has led to violent reactions. It's like having something on the tip of your tongue every blessed second of every blessed day, like the wisp of a memory or whatever, and not being able to fully articulate it because it eludes you over and over. I understand it can be maddening."

"Um, yeah," Bel snorted. "Hey, Stevie B? Remember that guy way back in the dark ages before we were excommunicated from the coven barbecues? Shoot, what was his name…"

I shivered hard, rubbing my arms. "Gibbon. Gibbon Martell. And holy leaping lizards, do I remember Gibbon. He's a perfectly good example of why not to possess a body."

"Stevie's right. Check this out, Arkady. We're all at the Fourth of July coven barbecue, right? Gibbon, somehow—we all still don't know how he pulled it off —came back from the dead and hopped into Judas Hall's body. We didn't know who was in Judas's skin until he attacked the man who was smooching on his wife…er, *Gibbon's* wife. She'd moved on a year or so after he'd kicked the bucket and found herself a new love. Gibbon, while in Judas's body, beat the poor guy to within an inch of his life. I had potato salad in my fur for days afterward. When Baba Yaga asked why Gibbon/Judas beat the guy up, despite knowing he'd end up in the slammer, he said he didn't know but there was a good reason, and it was *right on the tip of his tongue.*"

Arkady didn't say a word, but he did let out a whistling gasp.

"So not only did they expel his spirit from Judas's body and shun his soul for attempted murder, and for possessing a body by means of witchcraft for personal gain, he was sent off to oblivion for beating up a guy over a woman he doesn't even remember. How do ya like them apples?"

"So you say Zero might forget us? *Forever?*" He squeaked the word, his normally husky voice climbing a couple of octaves.

The mere thought had me close to tears, and I would not cry. There was no time for tears. "It's just one of the possibilities, Arkady. One of several. There could be glitches in the new host body if the spirit isn't a good fit. He could struggle to sustain the host body. He could forget how to walk or talk or all sorts of things."

"But he has done before, *dah?* He has been in other body two times now," Arkady reminded me.

I let my head hang low, stretching out my neck. "He has, but he's never been able to stay in the body..."

"But hold on, that could be for various reasons,

Boss. Could be it was the wrong body and he knew it, so he aborted the mission."

While that was true, I didn't know if it was Win's truth. "You're right. That could be."

My voice must have lost its conviction and gone soft as I listed all the things that could go wrong, because Arkady instantly soothed me.

"You must not think worst. But you must sleep, *malutka*. You are exhausted." He clapped his hands, a sharp, jolting action that made me jump. "Now, off to bed with you, little rosebud. Tomorrow is new day. Tomorrow we find Zero."

"Okay, okay. I'll get some rest," I conceded, even though I was sure I wouldn't sleep a wink. "But before I do, did you ask around again? Double check with everyone up there to see if they've seen him?"

"Of course I check, my petunia, and while you take nap, I ask again. But I insist right now you rest. *Please.* We need you strong like bull, *dah*?"

He was right. I'd be no good to anyone if I didn't rest my whirring mind. Win wouldn't like it if he found out I hadn't banked as many hours of sleep as I could before things went sideways. He always said resting during the calm was prudent for the storm.

I'm not sure why I had a gut feeling everything was going to turn to chaos. It's not like we'd heard anything in the last twenty-four hours. I just knew it would.

Calling Whiskey, I nodded as I made my way out of the kitchen and toward the stairs, plodding upward with weary steps. My heart was heavy, but my resolve was still intact.

If Win hadn't crossed over, he was out there. Somewhere. But where? What if I hadn't checked a big enough radius for reported deaths? What if the body he'd deemed worthy was in Sri Lanka? Or worse, what if the death of the host hadn't been reported at all? The host body could be jacked up in some dark alley or left to rot in a dirty Dumpster.

Stop, Stephania. I could almost hear Win in my ear reprimanding me for all the "what ifs" I was calling to mind. I had to stop creating scenarios that didn't yet exist and stick to the facts.

The only thing I knew for certain was this: I wouldn't give up until I had an answer for his disappearance. Nothing would stop me from looking for him—even if it took a lifetime.

Trudging into my bedroom, I felt the potential for defeat gnaw at my gut. Fear and defeat. I had to narrow this search somehow. There were too many variables.

As I kicked off my shoes and unwrapped the scarf around my neck, I headed to the bathroom to wash my face and brush my teeth.

And that was when I saw the message written in my favorite lipstick on the mirror above my sink.

Look 4 bath.

CHAPTER 6

" *L*ook for bath?" Arkady repeated in obvious confusion over the message left by heaven only knew. "Arkady Bagrov does not understand. Zero want you to find bathroom? What the heckles?"

I blinked under the warm lighting of the bathroom and tried to make heads or tails of this new message. The writing was choppy and partially in cursive, definitely a lost art these days, and quite possibly from someone older.

The two O's in the word "look" were smushed together, and the word "bath" used the less common way to write the letter A. Rather than make a circle with the tail on the bottom and to the right, the small A had the hook at the top, facing left, and reminded me of the more traditional handwriting taught decades ago.

Yet, they'd used the number four instead of the word—which was very current and more in the style of a text. Did that mean whoever had written it had been in a hurry? Was it some confused ghost who straddled the line between generations and had a good grasp on both old and new styles?

Gripping the cool porcelain of my bathtub, I sat down on the edge and stared mindlessly at the assorted loofah sponges and bath bombs in a basket on the windowsill, feeling as though the wind had been knocked out of me.

"Stevie?" Bel tweeted at me as he flew to the basket's handle and perched there. "Don't drift off without taking us with you. Let's talk this out."

I exhaled and looked at the message again. "Okay, so first, *who* wrote that? Was it a spirit from the after-life, or Win himself? Can he even write things? Arkady? Do you know?"

If so, he'd never done it around me. I do know he's moved an object or two on occasion, but nothing monumental. Had he been hiding his abilities from me for the express purpose of this stunt?

I'd always thought Win and I were mostly open books ever since he'd told me about the night he died, but if he knew I'd disapprove because it was incredibly unsafe, he would have kept this from me. I was sure of that.

"I do not know. He has never done this with Arkady. I have only do once. Remember? But it was in Japanese. Everything went kaplooey."

Nodding slowly, I said, "I do remember. We were investigating the Chef Le June murder, right? It had to do with something about the guy fixing the heating vent?"

"*Dah.* Your house was still under construction and I was practicing on wall. The worker man see what I write."

I laughed softly. "I remember Win's exact words on the subject. 'You made him think he was seeing things'," I said in my imitation of Win's accent. "I remember him telling us the poor man went to see a neurologist because he thought he was losing his marbles."

"Oh, yeah!" Bel agreed. "I remember you guys telling me about that. So you think this could be Win's work? And what do you think it means, Stevie? Is it some secret spy code? You know, like Morse code but not?"

I stared at the message in red again and shook my head. "Arkady? Thoughts? Is this some kind of crazy spy-speak?"

"I do not understand what this message means, *malutka.* If it is some secret code, it is nothing Arkady understands." He paused and then he said, "This message have to be about Zero. Too many coincidences at once for it to be anything else. "

But was the message *from* Zero or only *about* him? Was he communicating with us personally, or had he sent someone in his stead? I wouldn't doubt Win could charm the knickers right off another ghost and get them to do whatever he wanted

Rising, I went to the sink where my lipstick sat on

the shelf beneath the gorgeous oval mirror framed in whitewashed wood, sitting there just as I'd left it this morning.

Nothing was amiss. Nothing was moved.

"Argh!" I yelled, shaking a fist at the ceiling. "What's happening, Win? What are you trying to tell me?"

Bel flew to my shoulder and whispered, "There, there, Stevie. Ease up a little and let's keep talking this through. We're not without clues. We have rebirth, imposter, and now bath. Let's put our heads together and think."

As I was about to do that, I remembered the metal box of papers I had stashed in my walk-in closet. I jabbed a finger in the air. "Hold that thought, guys," I said as I made a break for the closet, unfolding the stepladder so I could reach the top shelf.

Grabbing the heavy box, I dragged it from the shelf and hopped off the ladder, placing it on the lush carpet of the closet floor—carpet Win insisted I have to keep my feet warm in the winter.

"*Malutka*? What are you doing?"

I tapped the top of the box with a fingernail and flipped it open. "The papers from Win's lawyer have to be signed, right? As a for instance, his will where he left everything to me, right?"

Bel flew into the closet, landing on the floor. As he waddled toward me, his round body swaying to and fro, he said, "Uh, okay, and what will that mean, Stevie?"

I grabbed the envelope with the will and held it up

in victory, forcing my eyes away from the picture of Win with Miranda in Paris and shouted, "We can compare handwriting!"

"Bravo, *malutka!*" Arkady cheered as I scurried back to the bathroom mirror and eyeballed the message.

I pulled the official-looking paper from the envelope and held it up near the writing on the mirror. Unfortunately, most of the letters that matched one another in his signature and the message—as in the case of the A and the L—were opposites. Little A's versus a cap, and vice versa.

Now, the letter O in "Winterbottom" and "look" might be another story...

I squinted and looked harder. "See the letter O, Arkady? It has that little squiggly loop on top. Could be a possible match, don't you think?"

"Ummm... I am no handwriting expert, sugarsnap, but I—"

"Don't think so," Bel said dryly. "They look nothing alike, Stevie, and you know it. Now you're creating narratives that don't exist. What does Win always say about that?"

"Don't chase shadows." I repeated his familiar words numbly. "Stick to the facts."

Belfry clucked his tongue. "Riiight. It's a waste of time, and the fact is, the handwriting looks nothing like Win's. I bet if you look at some of the other signatures on that tome of a will, you'll see I'm right."

I closed my eyes and took deep breaths before I

stuffed the will back in the envelope. "You're right. I'm reaching."

"I'll say, but that doesn't mean you shouldn't *keep* reaching until you latch on to something solid, Stevie. Now, you need sleep. We've beaten this to death for the moment, and we're on the fast train to nowhere. Wash up. It's bedtime for all ex-witches."

"Do you promise to wake me if you hear anything, Arkady? Swear? There are no boundaries now, okay?" We had limits about things like bedtime and bathroom usage, and neither Win nor Arkady had ever broken the rules, but rules be damned.

I needed to know where Win was.

"Of course, *malutka*. If I hear anything, I will wake you right away. I promise this."

My shoulders slumped at the thought of halting our search, but I put the envelope back and went about my nightly routine as though everything were normal—because at that point, I still refused to believe it never would be again.

~

*S*omehow, I managed to grab some shuteye, but it was littered with dreams of Win, a kaleidoscope of him in different settings. The way I see him in my mind when he tells me about one of his missions, and even with Miranda at the Eiffel Tower.

Needless to say, it wasn't very restful, but it was

better than nothing. I certainly wasn't refreshed, but I was better than I'd been last night.

Throwing my legs over the side of the bed, I stroked Whiskey's head and looked at the picture in the frame I'd bought, sitting on my nightstand. The picture frame housed a photo of some random model. I'd once used it to tease Win when I had no idea what he looked like. I told him it gave me a frame of reference—little did I know how closely he resembled the man in the picture.

The dark-haired, blue-eyed, handsome-as-the-devil model in the photo, I'd come to find, almost freakishly resembled Win. Sometimes when we were chatting, and I wanted to really stir him up, I'd pretend the picture in the frame was Win. It's been was our little joke since nearly day one.

Seeing it now, my heart clenched and constricted until I thought it would burst through the wall of my chest.

I traced the outline of the model's jaw, something I'd done when I was alone many times before as I wondered what it would be like to have Win physically here with us. I whispered, *"Where are you?"*

Closing my eyes, I sent out a prayer to the universe that something—anything—would happen today that would give us a hint, before I hopped down to the floor.

As I raced into the bathroom because I couldn't stay in bed any longer or I'd go mad, Bel was already up, setting out my toothbrush with some toothpaste (I know it sounds crazy, but his wee hands are quite adept). "Mornin', Stevie."

"No time, Bel. Have to get a move on," I said, heading back out and dismissing him without thinking about how rude that was.

"*Excuuuse me,* but you will march your sassy pants right back in there and brush your teeth and shower, little lady!" he demanded as he buzzed in front of my face, his eyes flashing angry orders. "Win's disappearance is not a good enough excuse for poor hygiene, miss. Now get. I'll start the shower."

I sighed like I used to when I was eight or nine, and he'd given me my marching orders, but then I smiled. "Thanks for reminding me a clean spy is a useful spy," I teased, feeling better already as I picked up the toothbrush—

Only to stop dead in my tracks.

The mirror was clean.

No! We needed that message. It was a clue!

But Belfry was in my ear in an instant. "Relax, Nancy Drew. I took a picture of it with your phone, which weighs as much as an elephant, FYI. I got your back. Now go brush your teeth. Your breath smells like toxic waste."

I blew out a breath I didn't know I was holding and smiled into the mirror, my eyes round and glassy from lack of sleep but, I noted, still determined. "Thanks, Bel." I turned back to the task of brushing and focused on a plan. Win said we should always have a plan.

Today we would find Win. That was the plan.

But you know what they say about plans and intentions—or is that roads? I don't know. I can't remember anymore. I only know whoever said it, they understood hell.

Because this was, indeed, hell.

Another almost ten solid hours and a shower later, my optimism and my plan had begun to fade, and fade fast.

Leaning over the kitchen island, I pressed my palms against the edge of the cool marble and arched my back, stretching the muscles. I was on E at this point. We'd been tearing through room after room, looking for any kind of clue, and if you know Mayhem Manor, you know it has endless rooms and more storage spaces than The Container Store.

We'd decided our plan of attack was to go over the house with a fine-tooth comb, looking for clues possibly sent by Win.

I'd been hopeful this morning. Now that it was almost time for dinner and my arms and legs were sore from crawling in and out of tight spaces and hauling storage boxes around? Not so much.

"You look in garage, yes?" Arkady asked for the umpteenth time, making me clench my teeth to keep from screaming my anguish and frustration.

"Yes. I looked in every tote, every box, every stinkin' drawer in the storage bins three times. There's nothing, Arkady. Absolutely nothing."

We'd never had an instance when obvious, visible signs were sent to us without Win to interpret the meaning—or at least ask the sender. So we'd decided Spy Guy was responsible for trying to get a message to us about his location, because we really didn't have anything else to go on and we had to choose a path.

We chose the one where Win stalks us from the afterlife. Or, maybe to better describe it, we chose the path where our man of mystery sends some errant spirit to stalk us; one who makes absolutely no sense and is incapable of finishing a sentence.

Planting my hands on my hips, I scrunched my eyes shut and thought—I thought hard. If I were a clue to Win's whereabouts, where would I be?

"The attic?" Belfry asked as though he'd read my mind.

I swiped a finger in the air. "It's the only place we haven't looked. And as a by the by, we haven't really accumulated as much as you'd think after two years. Shouldn't we have way more junk?"

"If you remember right, we didn't start with much junk to begin with, Stevie. It was mostly the clothes on our back after that dusty old hag shipped us off from Paris."

My smile was a wry one as I remembered how little we'd truly had, and how full up everything had become because of Win. Tears stung my eyes, and I had to grit my teeth to stop a sudden onslaught. No way was I breaking down now.

Something was going on here and I knew it had to do with Win. That was the only incentive I needed to keep my act together.

"And look at what we have now, huh?" I said, trying to keep my voice even.

"We've come a long way, haven't we, Boss?" Belfry murmured from Whiskey's back.

"We sure have, buddy."

"So…the attic?"

"The attic it is!" I said, jetting down the hall to the staircase, Whiskey in tow.

Running up the stairs, I ignored how wobbly I was or how rubbery my muscles felt, because I had a new mission and that meant hope. But the ring of the doorbell stopped me cold.

I wasn't expecting anyone, and Dana and Melba always gave me a heads up before they dropped by. It couldn't be Chester, either—not unless he'd decided to give up his *Wheel of Fortune* and his warm slippers.

Zooming back down the stairs, I was instantly on alert. We'd already had one run-in with a violent ghost. I didn't cherish the idea of another.

I looked at the security camera and cocked my head.

It was Cory from the local pizza place, holding a small square box of pizza. He was new, and a really nice kid, but he definitely had the wrong house.

As I stared at his lanky frame on the doorbell cam, his bleached-blond hair with the dark roots blowing in the heavy wind, I narrowed my eyes.

"Bel? Did you order a pizza for me?" I whispered.

"Nope. I planned on making you heat up the leftover grilled chicken and broccoli from Carmella because you need something in that belly. No pizza orders here, Boss."

Instantly, I became suspicious. As we well know, a delivery guy who turned out to be a murderer had fooled me once before. It's the very reason I have the camera to begin with. Win insisted upon it.

That would not happen again.

Nope. Not today, Satan.

While I know Cory vaguely, I can't say for sure he couldn't be bribed to deliver something nefarious, and seeing as Win was missing and all manner of strange things were happening, my suspicion grew.

I pressed the button for the security camera and asked, "Hey, Cory! What's up?"

He held up the pizza, smiling his infectious grin, complete with deep dimples and twinkling blue eyes. "Delivery, Miss Cartwright."

"But I didn't order a pizza, Cory."

He appeared puzzled as he looked down at the receipt. "Has your name and address on it. I heard the guy back at the store take the order."

At this point in the day, after having only a Twinkie for breakfast and skipping lunch entirely in favor of scouring the house for clues, maybe I shouldn't look a gift horse in the mouth.

Speaking of mouths, mine began to water at the idea of pizza. "Can I see it?"

Cory gave me a confused look. "Sure, Miss Cartwright. Hey, you okay?" he asked as he pulled the box from the insulated bag and flipped the top open.

Pepperoni and mushroom. My favorite. Now I was more curious than anything else, so I popped the door open and smiled at him. "I'm fine, Cory. I just wondered if whoever sent this to me knows what I like." Taking the box from him and setting it on the table by the stairs, I grabbed my purse and dug around for some cash. "What do I owe you?"

He shrugged, tucking the bag under his arm. "Nothin'. Whoever ordered it paid for it already."

Alarm bells shot off in my head as the wind whooshed into the entryway, making me shiver. "Really? Credit card? Debit?"

Cory stared at me as the rain battered the front porch and the wind raged. "Not sure. But you can probably call the store and ask."

Handing him a five-dollar bill, I smiled again. "I'll do that, and thanks. I'm actually starving."

"Okey-doke, Miss Cartwright. Enjoy your dinner," he said with a wave as he scooted down the steps and toward the driveway to his compact car.

Closing the door on the cold wind, I scratched my head and stared at the pizza. "Weird, huh, guys?"

"*Malutka*, you smell before you eat, yes? One time, when I am in bowels of Laos on mission, bad lady tried to poison me. I would not know if I did not use nose first."

Belfry barked a laugh. "That bad lady was your third ex-wife, buddy, and from what you told us, you deserved to be poisoned, you old coot. You told us that story on poker night. Try again, Boo."

I took the pizza and headed back to the kitchen, my legs tired and my arms sore. "You guys have a poker night? How didn't I know about this?"

"You get mani/pedis and hang out with Melba at the thrift store, we play poker. We're allowed to have lives outside of you, aren't we?"

I giggled, and it felt good to release some of my tension. Grabbing my cell, I dialed up the pizza place. "But poker? I didn't even know you knew how to play poker, Bel." As the phone rang, I popped open the box, savoring the saucy smell of cheese and pepperoni.

"Petey's Pizza!" a feminine voice chirped cheerfully in my ear.

I paced my way to the windows by the kitchen table and stared out into the rainy darkness. "Hello, this is Stevie Cartwright. Your delivery guy Cory just dropped off a pizza to me."

"Yep! The deep dish, right? Is something wrong?"

"No, no. Absolutely not. I was just wondering if you could tell me who ordered it, because I didn't."

There was a small pause and some clicking, and then the youthful voice said, "But you did, Miss Cartwright. You used your credit card, the one we have on file here."

CHAPTER 7

I know the blood drained from my face because my nose went cold, along with the rest of my limbs. This had to be a message from Win. What else could it be?

"So the order was called in?"

"Yes, ma'am," she answered, perky and light.

"And the person said it was me?"

I heard the flipping of papers and then, "That's what it says. Is there anything else I can help you with, Miss Cartwright?"

Thanking the girl after explaining away the mix-up, I hung up and stared harder at the pizza as I made my way back across the kitchen.

Bel flew to the counter and landed by the box. "This is cuckoo, Stevie. Plain old nuts."

"*Dah.* Wing-ed one is right. I do not understand this. Not one bit."

"You and me both," I commented, pulling a piece of

the pizza from the box, inhaling the scent of gooey cheese, saucy meat, and mushrooms.

Then I frowned when I looked at it again. "I don't think this is from Win. It's deep dish, guys. Win knows I like thin crust. Not that it'll stop me, because I'm starving, but this can't be from Spy Guy."

"Then who's ordering you a pizza?" Bel asked dryly. "With your favorite toppings?"

As I took my first bite, which was delicious despite the thick crust, and made my way to the pantry to grab food for Whiskey and Strike, I shook my head. "That is curious. I mean, it's not like I hide the fact that I like mushrooms and pepperoni on my pizza. It's not a matter of national security, but who would imper-sonate me to order a pizza *for me*? It has to be Win. He has to have found a way to get through to us. What worries me is, if he's going to attempt to hop into a body, and he succeeds but we're not there to help him, anything could happen."

My stomach rolled at the thought. As I said before, if he doesn't remember who he is or was before he body hopped, he could end up in a world of trouble with no one to claim him, and that terrified me.

Bel flapped his wings. "Then we keep working under the assumption all the weird stuff going on around here is Winterbutt, or somebody helping Winterbutt, and we proceed as necessary. No way I'm going to let my buddy down if I can help it."

Belfry and his loyalty never failed to make my heart warm. So I nodded my consent. "Okay, let's go over this again, yes? I feel like we're missing something, and if we find that something, maybe we'll figure out the reason for the pizza. What do we have so far?"

"Imposter, rebirth, look for bath, and pizza. Deep-dish pizza, my jalapeno pepper," Arkady ticked the list off.

I'd laugh if I didn't want so much to cry, so I took another bite of the pizza before saying, "None of which makes any sense at all. Maybe there's a clue missing? And why the heck is he sending us these disjointed clues? Wouldn't it be easier if he had someone write something like, 'Hey! I'm in Peoria. I need a ride home' on the bathroom mirror instead of these half sentences and random items? I mean, what the heck does a deep-dish pizza mean anyway?"

"Where is this Peoria, *malutka*?"

I giggled and carried Whiskey's bowl of kibble out to the kitchen, shoving the last of the crust in my mouth and reaching for another piece. "It's not important, it was just an example. Here's what's important, why is Win doing such a hatchet job on these clues?" Then I paused and, once more, said something I didn't want to believe, but for posterity's sake, needed to be said. "Or…maybe it's not Win at all…"

I dreaded that notion more than anything else. If this wasn't Win, then the only connection I had with him would be gone. The nothingness of that made my heart ache.

"Of course it is Zero, Stevie. Of course it is," Arkady said, but he didn't sound at all convinced.

I looked up at the ceiling, my pizza suddenly tasting like cardboard. "Then why does it sound like you're convincing yourself?"

Arkady's silence said everything and nothing. He wasn't so sure it was Win anymore, either.

I dropped the remainder of the slice on a napkin on the counter. "The pizza's the clincher for me, too, Arkady. It's thrown me off his scent. He knows what kind of crust I like. It's the one glitch in our giddyup."

"But that doesn't mean the pizza doesn't mean something. It doesn't mean Win's not trying to tell us something, Stevie. I'd bet my knickers this pizza means something important. So let's break it down. Imposter means...?" Belfry coaxed in a hopeful tone.

I shrugged my shoulders, my thoughts growing fuzzier by the minute as I grew more tired. "It has to mean Win. He played roles throughout his career. Being a spy means he had to pretend to be other people. That's an easy one."

"Right," Bel confirmed. "Rebirth means he's hopping into a body and hopes to be reborn. That one's easy, too. Next up is *look for bath*, which makes zero sense. I can't even tie it to the other two clues."

I ran my hands through my hair in sheer frustration. "Me either. But he did write it in the bathroom. Wait..." I muttered before my head popped up and a shot of adrenaline hit me. "Maybe there's something in the bathroom? In the drain? How could he get something in the drain?"

I knew I was grasping at straws, but I'd try anything at this point, even if it meant taking some pipes apart.

"Maybe same way he do the rest? With help from spirits?" Arkady asked.

Slapping my clammy hands against my thighs, I shook my head. "But what spirits, Arkady? Where? What plane is he on and how the heck is he getting all this help?"

Now Arkady laughed. "One thing to know about Zero, he is very charming gentleman. If he can talk Mesopotamian Prince into giving up his spare palace in negotiation talks with cranky Saudi Arabian, he can do anything. Ooo-wee, that was bad, bad time. But he do it. The man, he is genius."

I grinned. That was my Win. "Okay. So he's good at talking people into doing things. No surprise. But spirits are a different breed altogether. They don't always work or think the way people here on Earth do. They're usually confused and disoriented."

"I am not confused," Arkady defended with attitude.

"But you're a rarity. So is Win, for that matter. Still, knowing Win, maybe it's not impossible. All that aside, it leaves our latest clue. Pizza."

"Yeah. Pizza," Belfry said into the silence. "Pizza with toppings you like and a crust you hate. If this clue is from Win, I'm telling you, when I get my hands on him, I'm going to give him bloody what for. All this indirect, run-around-the-mulberry-bush nonsense is for the birds."

Would we ever get our hands on him again? I

sighed as I began to head upstairs. "You and me both. All right, c'mon, guys. We have a drain to pull apart and an attic to canvass."

I sent out a prayer to the universe that we'd find something, just a tiny hint, because I had this dreadful feeling deep in my gut we were running out of time.

Have I mentioned I hate my gut today?

~

I sat amidst the many fittings and pipes involved in putting together a sink (who knew it took so many?) and a bathtub and leaned my head back against the front of the toilet, and I didn't even care if that was gross.

I was depleted.

"You're exhausted, Stevie. You need to recharge," Bel encouraged, as he wisped his wings over my face, brushing my bird's nest of hair out of my eyes.

I held up the monkey wrench I'd used to bend one particular pipe to my will by beating it until it came apart, and shook my head. "I won't sleep, so I might as well be productive."

"This is mess, *malutka*. This is not productive."

I had to agree with him, the bathroom was a mess, and so was the attic, and we had nothing to show for it but a huge hairball and one of my earrings. "You're right. It is a mess. I'd better get it cleaned up."

"Oh, no. You'd better go to bed, or at the very least rest your overtired body, Stevie. It's really late."

Using my hands to push myself off the floor, I began moving things that looked similar into piles. Gosh, Enzo was going to have a cow when he saw this, and of course, there'd be questions about why I'd torn the bathroom apart.

I hiked up my sweats and eyeballed the tub, the bottom of it currently housing a lot of the hardware I'd pulled apart. "I guess I'm going to have to ask Enzo to come in and fix this, huh?"

"If you ever want to take a shower in here again. Good thing we have four other bathrooms. Now let's go to bed, Stevie. Please. You can't be at your best if you're not rested. We've been at this for two days straight with only a small break in between. Bedtime. Now," Bel ordered in that authoritative tone he'd been using a lot of these past couple of days.

"Yes, chicken and dumplings, I must agree with wee wing-ed one. You look like cat drag you. Remember what we spies always say, rest when you can. Now is time."

I waved a dismissive hand as my mind raced. If only I *could* rest, but despite my exhaustion, my body was a bunch of nerve endings all on fire. My inner turmoil was at its peak. The longer Win was silent, the farther away he felt.

Save the imposter.

The words kept running through my mind like an Indy racecar. I hadn't voiced my fears about that particular phrase yet, but if this really was Win sending the messages to us, it meant he knew he needed to be saved.

"Tell me what you're thinking, Stevie," Bel insisted, landing on my shoulder to snuggle against my ear.

I sighed, and it was ragged and worn. Dropping the pipe into a pile, I steadied myself. "Those words. *Save the imposter.* Someone thinks Win needs saving…or maybe *Win* knows he needs saving."

"Or maybe it's all just jumbled-up information, Stevie. You know, the way spirits confuse stuff. You said so yourself."

"But what if it isn't, Bel? What if he's in danger and he knows it and I can't find him to help?"

I felt the first chink in my armor, that subtle but clear nagging feeling that maybe I'd never see Win again.

I'd ignored it so far. I'd dismissed it and tucked it away somewhere in the deep recesses of my mind to keep from dwelling on the worst possible scenario. But it was there, and tonight, when I was tired and feeling very alone without Win to help me solve this puzzle, it became magnified.

"We will find Zero, *malutka. We will,*" Arkady insisted, his voice sharp.

"Yep. We will," I agreed with a smile, injecting as much enthusiasm into my tone as possible when I really wasn't feeling it at all. "And now, I'm going to do as suggested and try to get some rest. So skedaddle, you two mother hens. I'm fine. Promise."

I felt anything but fine, but fake it 'til you make it,

right? So as I grabbed some pajamas, my toothbrush and my hand cream, and headed down our wide hall to the second of four bathrooms, absently looking at the framed art Win had personally chosen, I kept my chin up.

I wasn't going to give in to fear and supposition yet. Not yet.

After I'd brushed my teeth and washed my face, I trudged back to the bedroom where Whiskey waited patiently, sitting on the braided throw rug in the middle of the polished hardwood, wagging his tail and panting in that barely contained, excited way of his.

His big body rippled without moving, his velvety-soft fur ruffled and his eyes went wide.

Huh. He only did that when he was super happy to see someone, like Dana or Bel—or when he heard Win's voice...

A chill zipped along my spine as I knelt beside him. "Whiskey, buddy, what's got you so revved up?"

His chocolate-brown eyes stared upward at the nightstand, making me frown—

And then I popped up from the floor, reaching for the picture of the fake Win with trembling fingers, and gasped.

Someone—or maybe I should say, some *spirit*—had drawn a dark mustache on fake Win's picture.

And if I do say so myself, in the midst of all this turmoil, it was pretty darned hilarious.

CHAPTER 8

*O**M**y* mouth fell open in disbelief, and then I couldn't help but giggle because the mustache, as crudely drawn as it was, truly looked pretty funny. It resembled, in a kindergarten kind of way, the sort a villain in a cartoon would twirl while he cackled evilly.

A villain...

Was that what he was trying to tell me? There was a villain involved? Or was that another one of my reaches?

Whiskey pawed my thigh, the excitement he'd managed to keep at bay before now gone. When he pawed my leg, it meant he was ready for sleep, and I should be, too.

I sat on the edge of the bed and patted it, indicating he should hop up. "If only you could talk like the rest of this ragtag bunch, huh, buddy? Is Timmy in the well? Is that what all that quivering excitement was about?" I asked, staring into the deep pools of his soft eyes.

But he only licked my hand and moved to the end of the bed, where he stretched out his lumbering body and closed his eyes.

"You decent?" Belfry called from the hallway.

"Define that word when referring to me," I quipped, hoping to keep my continually rising anxiety to myself by deflecting with jokes.

"Always a funny girl," he retorted, flying into my room to land on the bed.

"What's up?" I asked as I crawled under my thick comforter.

"Nothing. I'm just checking on you. That's what familiars do. They hover and annoy and in general make sure their charges are taking care of themselves."

I smiled, staring out the round window next to my built-in bed at the foggy night. "Look at the picture of fake Win and tell me what you see."

There was a light pause, and then he harrumphed. "What the hasenpfeffer's going on? Is that a clue? What kind of clue is that, for the love of kiwis?"

I closed my tired, grainy eyes and moved my head from side to side. "I don't know. When I came into the bedroom, Whiskey was behaving strangely. You know, doing that excited thing he does when Dana or Enzo drop by. Or like when Win speaks to him…"

"Do you think Win was here, that he did this?" he squeaked, zipping around the room. "But how, Stevie?"

"*Something* was here, Bel. Something Whiskey

wasn't at all apprehensive about. Was it Win? No clue. But we know for sure it wasn't Dana or Enzo. If Win found a way to appear as a spirit, I couldn't see it, right? Because I can't see or hear them anymore, but maybe Whiskey can."

"So I suppose you want to dissect this? Analyze it until our eyeballs cross?"

What I really wanted was some time to myself to do those things. I needed a break from everyone telling me I needed to rest.

"There's nothing to discuss, really. It's kind of a shoddy clue, don't you think?" I looked up at the ceiling and shook my finger. "Hear that, Spy Guy? If you're hovering around here somewhere, Win, I hope you heard that. Your clues stink!"

Both Bel and I sat silent for a few seconds before he asked again, "You sure you don't want to talk it out?"

I wondered if I should mention the bit about the villain mustache, but decided against it. One of us anxious was enough. "I think I'm too tired to dissect."

Hopping onto my chest, Belfry looked down at me with his thickly lashed eyes (I'm so jealous of his eyelashes. They really are long and thick. Wasted on a bat, if you ask me) and sighed. "I can't figure this out, Stevie. I just don't get it. The only thing I *do* get is Win would never leave you unless he was taken or there was a good reason. Period. There's no in between."

I swallowed hard, my eyes burning. Those notions aside, there was something weighing far heavier on my mind than pizza and body hopping, and I had to share before I burst.

"Bel?"

"Yeah, Boss?"

"What if…" I inhaled and exhaled to keep my fleeting composure in check. "What if he really is… gone, and I didn't tell him how…how I feel?"

"Don't you think he knew, Stevie?" Belfry asked softly, his voice hushed and gentle.

How could he? I'd never spoken a word about it to him. "I don't know. I never said…"

"Because you didn't want him to feel any pressure to stay on Plane Limbo if what he really wanted was to cross. I know that, Goose."

My throat ached with the threat of tears I fought to keep at bay. "I never believed something like this was even a possibility. Not a real one, anyway. I mean, I know body surfing happens, but it's so rare. I should have known Win would find a way. But I didn't want him to stay on Plane Limbo if crossing over was what his heart told him to do."

"You're a good soul, Stevie. You've always been kind and thoughtful, but I need you to trust me on what I'm about to say, okay?"

"Okay," I whispered into the darkness as a hot tear slipped from the corner of my eye.

"Win knew. He knew, and for the same reasons you didn't tell him, he didn't tell you how *he* felt, either."

"I wish…"

"I know, Stevie," he murmured, brushing my cheek with his wing.

"If I ever get the chance, caution be darned, I'm going to tell him, Bel." I whispered the promise to myself.

I vowed right then and there the next time I heard or, with any luck, saw Win, I was going to spew my guts up—I was going to tell him everything in my heart.

Everything.

"Good girl, but for right now—because Arkady's right, you *do* look like something the cat dragged in—please try to get some rest and we'll start fresh tomorrow. Do it for me."

I snuggled down farther under the comforter and half-closed my eyes, knowing full well I wouldn't sleep, but aiming to appease Bel. "I'll try. Now, off you go." Pressing a kiss to my fingers, I touched his snout before I felt him hop off my chest to go to bed.

Now, in my defense, I did try to sleep. I stared out the window. I stared at the ceiling of my fabulous bed. I counted bats (Belfry always thought that was more fun than sheep), and I changed positions at least a hundred times before I gave up.

It was one of those nights where every little itch rose to the surface of my skin and my pajamas kept twisting around my body, leaving me uncomfortable. I was too hot then I was too cold. I was overthinking every conversation I'd ever had with Win.

I was sick with my stupidity for not telling him how

deeply I cared for him, the heck with the consequences. But that niggle of fear, not just over our unconventional living conditions, but fear of rejection, had kept my lips sealed.

No more. I was going to dive in the deep end the first chance I got.

Anyway, sleep was elusive. So I gave up and tiptoed out of my bedroom, taking the picture of fake Win with me and heading downstairs to scour the Internet for more death notifications in the immediate vicinity.

I guess I didn't realize how long I'd been sitting by the cold fireplace in the living room, laptop on my knees, because before I knew it, the cold, rainy night turned into a cold, rainy day.

I'd spent an entire night and early morning Internet surfing, looking up everything from death notices to articles on MI6. I don't know what I'd hoped to achieve, but if sleep wasn't an option, aimlessly surfing the web was better than this hopeless pit.

"*Stevie!*" Belfry yelled from the stairwell as Whiskey thumped down the steps, making me jump.

Uh-oh. Caught.

"Morning, Belfry!" I said with exaggerated cheer. "How'd you sleep?"

He whizzed into the living room, fluttering in front of me while Whiskey watched. "Don't you good morning me, you faker! You haven't slept at all, have you?"

"I catnapped," I said, crossing my fingers.

"You didn't. You're lying to me. Know how I know

you're lying to me? Never mind. Don't answer. I'll tell you. You have so many bags under your eyes, you look like the baggage claim at JFK. How can you spy if you don't get some sleep? What good will you be to Win if you're not rested?"

Setting the laptop on the coffee table, I pinched the bridge of my nose. "What good will I be if we don't find him, Bel?" I said between clenched teeth, my patience, just like everything but my butt, beginning to wear thin.

"What good will you be when you do, and you can't keep your eyes open long enough to confess your deepest desires?" he taunted as I rose from the couch and headed to the kitchen for coffee.

"Never you mind about my deepest desires," I grumbled, agitated and about as cranky as I could ever remember being.

"*Malutka?* Why you do not call for Arkady to keep you company while you sit up all night alone?"

I grabbed a coffee pod and popped it into the Keurig, pressing the button and letting the heady scent of the nectar of the gods permeate my nose. "Because this is exhausting and you needed a break. *I* needed a break. I just needed some time to myself."

Opening a cabinet, I pulled out a mug—the one Win had Belfry buy for me for my birthday that reads, "First I drink the coffee. Then I do the things"—and drummed my fingers on the countertop with impatience. "So any news up there?" I asked hopefully, almost knowing that hope would be crushed.

"*Nyet*, cinnamon bun," Arkady answered softly.

As I headed to the pantry to fill Whiskey's bowl, with Strike following close behind, I happened upon a can of jellied cranberry sitting on the many shelves we'd had installed, one of my favorites at Thanksgiving, but, as per Win, more Philistine food. *Cranberry should be a chutney, not a jelly*, he'd said in his refined accent.

But seeing the can reminded me, we had a houseful of people coming the day after tomorrow, with no Win in sight. Not to mention, caterers.

"Thanksgiving dinner, Bel," I muttered as I filled Whiskey's bowl. "We need to cancel it. Even if we find Win, we won't be prepared, and it's not fair to keep people from making other arrangements. Bel? Can you handle it? Call the caterers so they can at least give the waiters notice. Have them donate the food to the shelter and the senior center, would you?"

"And what would you like me to tell everyone else?"

Tightening the belt on my fuzzy purple bathrobe, I gulped. "I'll call them myself. I have to convince them I have a family emergency, and it'll sound better coming from me than my virtual assistant."

It had been Bel's idea to call himself my virtual assistant, thus making the scheduling of appointments at Madam Zoltar's, among many other things, so much easier. But canceling Thanksgiving needed a personal touch. I also had to find a way to prevent Carmella from bringing me a casserole, which would be her first instinct if I didn't reassure her I had plenty of food.

"What about Mommy dearest and your father?" he asked. "Were they still coming or are they off globe-trotting?"

I reached for the necklace my father had given me, still around my neck, and smiled. He'd told me to use it if I ever needed him, and as vain and self-absorbed as he was, he'd step in and use his magic.

But I couldn't involve him in afterlife matters. He was a warlock, subject to the same rules as the rest of us, and that went for my mother, too.

We'd come a long way since the death of her latest husband, Bart, but there was no way I'd tell her about the mess I was in right now. She'd interfere on my behalf and Baba Yaga would have ten chickens. My mother had changed in many ways, but losing her powers because her daughter was in a pickle over a dead British spy wasn't on the agenda.

So I shook my head and sighed, almost wishing I could call them. "Neither of them were coming until Christmas. So we're okay there. Besides, they can't get involved, and you know they can't."

Bel flew out of the pantry and up to the ceiling toward the hallway. "Okey-doke, Boss. I'm on it," he called.

"Thanks, Bel." Wandering out of the pantry, I set Whiskey's bowl on the floor and scattered some seed for Strike, who clucked and cooed at my feet.

Grabbing my phone, I checked the time. It was only eight in the morning, too early to begin calling people.

I collected my cup of coffee and went to sit at the

kitchen table and watch the choppy waters of the Sound while I considered what was next. The wind slashed at the almost naked trees and rain pummeled our browning lawn, dripping off the plastic covers on our lawn furniture while I tried to think of a new plan of attack.

The gnawing ache in my heart and the turmoil in my stomach intensified then. I didn't know where to go from here, and I said so to Arkady.

"Arkady?"

But I was greeted with silence—a silence so silent, I froze.

"Arkady?" I whispered. "You there?" I cocked my head and listened, holding my breath.

Still—everything felt very still. Too still.

No. No, no, no! Had he done something stupid, like go looking for Win?

I rose from the table, almost knocking my coffee cup over. My muscles flexed and tensed, tightening in terror.

Clenching my fists, I banged on the table, frightening Strike and Whiskey, who both ran to the corner of the kitchen. "Arkady, answer me right now!"

Then I heard him sigh, a long, raspy bit of wind. "*Malutka*. We must speak."

I knew that tone. I knew that somber, ominous tone. Still, I steeled myself, gripping the edge of the table so hard, I thought my knuckles would crack. "Talk to me," was the best I could manage.

"I hear talk from spirit."

Closing my eyes, I licked my dry lips. "Talk?"

"*Dah.*"

My heart began that irregular thump inside my chest, and my skin went clammy and cold. I knew it wasn't good. I felt it way down inside, deep in my bones, and it made me yelp in frustration. "Just say it!"

"Sit, please, *malutka*. Sit before I tell you," Arkady begged, but I couldn't sit. I couldn't just sit and let it happen.

"Say it, Arkady!" I cried out as I began to pace. "Stop pussyfooting around and *say it!*"

"Spirit this morning say Zero…" He inhaled a harsh breath, one that whistled through my ears. "She say he…he cross to other side. She say he is gone for good."

CHAPTER 9

The blood drained from my face, and I had to grab the back of a chair to keep me standing as my legs wobbled.

"*Malutka...*" Arkady's tone was pleading and soft.

I held up a finger. I just needed a second to gather my thoughts. Just a second before this totally blank space in my head filled with questions. I knew they would come, but as Win would say, I was momentarily gobsmacked and I needed to catch my breath.

Bending at the waist, I breathed in and out, summoning all my strength and determination to help me face this.

Lifting my head, I gritted my teeth to keep from screaming. "Tell me exactly what happened, from the moment the spirit arrived to the moment she uttered those words. I need visuals and context, *please*."

"Just a moment ago, while you make plans to cancel fancy dinner, pretty lady spirit is talking to another spirit lady. They do this all the time, and we usually pay no mind. But today I listen because we need help to find our Zero. I really listen to everything."

Breathe, Stevie. Just breathe. "Tell me word for word what she said," I demanded, my head spinning.

He took another long pause, one that felt like a hundred years, but was surely only seconds. "She say... she say she see him go..."

"*Go?*" I forced the word out.

"*Dah*...into light," he answered, his words tight and choked with agonizing emotion.

I don't know what happened to me then, but I shifted into investigative mode. It was shaky and hesitant, but I fired off questions the same way I would if Arkady were a suspect in a murder. "Do you know this pretty lady spirit, Arkady? Did you ask her how she knew it was him? Did you ask her if she actually saw him cross or if that was just some afterlife gossip she quote-unquote heard? And lastly, when did this happen?"

I heard a nervous swallow before he finally said, "She know Zero, *malutka*. We see her all the time at waterfall. She know what Win look like. He is not hard to identify, Stevie. He is very distinct. Everyone know the handsome, charming dead spy. *Everyone*. I am telling you, she tell me she see him walk into light..."

The devastation that hit me square in my belly almost physically knocked me over. How could this be true? It couldn't be true! Win wouldn't leave without saying goodbye.

But when the light calls, Stevie, the spirit's destiny is to answer. I'd heard that a million times when I'd been in the business of mediums. The call was stronger than the desire to finish whatever business you've been hanging around waiting to finish.

If I listened to everything I'd ever heard about the light, the call was more than some siren's song, it was what was right and good and meant to be and the pull was the force of a million tidal waves.

Maybe Win had been resisting the light all this time because of me? Maybe what Bel said about the reasons I'd never confessed my feelings were true for Win, too? Maybe he shared my feelings and didn't reveal them for the same reasons I hadn't?

Maybe he finally realized the peril involved in body surfing and this time, when the light came calling, he'd ridden the wave to eternity?

Maybe rebirth meant moving on and being reborn in the light? I don't know what that had to do with the other clues, and if he did cross, how did he get spirits to send me clues to begin with? It had to have been premeditated. Yet still, that nagging feeling that wouldn't let go said if someone saw him leave, someone who could truly identify him... it made the most sense that he'd gone into the light

"Where is this spirit, Arkady? Where is she right now?"

He groaned in clear remorse. "She is gone, too, *malutka.* I cannot find her anywhere, but Arkady knows what he hears. He hear her say Zero is..."

"Gone." I threw the word because I couldn't contain it in me anymore. "Say it, Arkady!" I said, my voice rising. "He's gone!"

"Oh, my sweet corn fritter, I cannot say the word. I do not believe he would leave without saying goodbye. I cannot. *I will not!*" he thundered.

"Hey, you bunch of loudmouths, what the fudge is going on down here?" Bel asked as he flew back into the kitchen. "What's all the yelling about? I could hear you all the way up in the office on the other side of the house."

"Belfry—" Arkady began, but I cut him off before he could finish.

"Arkady heard a spirit talking this morning. She said she saw Win…" I clenched my teeth and spat the next words. "Go into the light."

Belfry didn't even bother to hide his gasp as he flew to the back of the chair I was still clinging to. "*What?* I don't believe it, Stevie! Arkady, are you sure?"

Arkady's response rang true with his misery. "I wish I did not hear, but this is what she say. I never tell you anything but truth, *malutka*. I never hurt you on purpose."

"I know that. I do. I—"

"Who is this *she*, Arkady?" Bel demanded.

"Stop yelling at him, Bel. It's not Arkady's fault he heard what he heard. She's a spirit on Plane Limbo," I replied, my response stiff, and don't think I didn't notice the change in my emotional state.

Because I did. Without warning, I felt like everything was happening around me, and even though I could hear the boys arguing with each other, it became muted.

I guess as the initial shock began to wear off, I'd gone numb. As I gathered up my coffee cup and brought it to the sink, I marveled at this strange, sudden calm. Gone was the jittery fear in my stomach. Gone was the incessant voice in my head telling me to figure out Win's disappearance.

"Belfry!" I heard Arkady yell with force. "You know Arkady would never hurt his *malutka*. We need facts, and if I hide this from her and it comes to be truth, then what? Then I am liar. Arkady Bagrov is no liar!"

"Weeell, we all know how reliable the spirits are, don't we? How many times have we gotten crossed wires from that motley bunch? More often than I can count on my fingers and toes. That's how many."

"You don't have toes. Or is it fingers?" I asked as Whiskey nudged my thigh for a scratch.

Bel's sigh was full of exasperation. "You know what I mean, Stevie. Things are confused up there every which way but Sunday. I'm not saying Arkady didn't hear what he says he heard. I'm just saying we can't be sure she saw Win cross, because half the time the spirits don't even know what their own names are."

Arkady confirmed, "*Dah*! What Belfry say is true. I pray that is what happen."

I held up my hands like white flags and shrugged, suddenly feeling quite tired. "Then where is he, Bel? We haven't gotten another clue since last night, and that mustache means about as much as the pizza in relation to Win. So where is he?"

"Mustache?" Arkady asked. "What is this you say?"

"Someone drew a mustache on that crazy picture Stevie has on her nightstand of the guy she thought Win looked like."

"When? When this happen, *malutka*?"

I trudged toward the hallway, almost in a hazy fog. "I guess last night while we were taking apart the bathroom pipes. It makes no sense. The only thing that does make sense is Win crossing over."

Bel buzzed right at my ear, his tone angry. "Then who's sending the messages, Stevie? If not Winterbutt, if he's really gone, then who? Why?"

I climbed the stairs, my feet moving without me feeling a thing as I clung to the banister. "Maybe someone's toying with me. Someone who knows I can no longer fight back. It's happened before."

"Stevie! Where are you going? If that's true, it someone's taunting you, we have to find out who it is. But most importantly, we need to find out if what this spirit said is true!" Bel yelled at me, zipping around my head with an audible flap of his wings.

I felt defeat weighing me down, oppressive and heavier each step I climbed. "I have to call everyone and cancel Thanksgiving, Bel. Then I'm going to get dressed."

"Oh, *malutka*. Arkady is sorry he make you so sad. I love you. You are my family when I have no one. I am responsible. How can I make right?"

I heard Arkady's agonized tone, heard the plea in his voice, but it was dulled. Rounding the corner, I went straight to my bedroom. "I know you would never hurt me intentionally, Arkady. I asked you to see what you could see, and you did, and I love you for it. This isn't your fault. Now, let me change and make those phone calls, okay?"

"And then we put heads together some more, *dah*?" he asked hopefully.

I began to close the door to my room, but before I did, I said, "Sure."

The hush of the door closing, the silence in my bedroom, the gloom of the day made me stand still and close my eyes, absorbing this abrupt and strange lack of panic.

I stared at fake Winterbottom's picture with his mustache, still without a clue as to who'd customized the photo. That should be driving me buggy, but I couldn't seem to put anything together.

All the tumult of the past three days, all the fear and anxiety fled, and I was left feeling dead inside.

That's exactly how I felt at that very moment.

Dead.

~

The entire day passed without me even noticing until Bel rapped sharply on my door. I'd never dressed after I'd made the necessary phone calls to cancel Thanksgiving dinner.

Instead, I'd plopped down in the chair in the corner of my room and watched the rain fall and the wind blow with no particular thoughts other than it was almost Thanksgiving, and I was grateful I wouldn't have a houseful of people for whom I'd have to pretend everything was fine.

"Stevie? Can I come in?"

My head popped up, and it was the first time since I'd come up here this morning that I took note of the time. It was almost eight o'clock...but what did the time really matter?

"Sure," I muttered, tucking my feet under me.

As he buzzed into the room, I watched him land on my nightstand with Whiskey in tow, who came to stand beside me, nosing my hand. Absently, I reached down and scratched his large head.

"Talk to me, Stevie. You've been up here for almost ten hours, just sitting. *Ten* hours. I flew around outside and looked in the window to check on you, and you haven't moved. What's happening?"

I stared blankly at him. "Nothing. I'm just sitting." Sitting and absorbing.

"That's shock, Stevie. You're numb from shock. You're protecting yourself from the pain. It's part of grieving. You know the signs. Now, come downstairs and I'll fix you something to eat and we'll talk. *Please*."

Maybe it was shock, but I can tell you this, it beat the unmerciful empty ache I'd had before. Still, I had the wherewithal to ask, "Hear anything from Win? Any new clues from above?"

Belfry sighed long and low, and I heard his regret when he answered. "No. Nothing. Nothing from upstairs, according to Arkady."

Nodding, I twisted the buttons on my pajamas.

"Stevie, I'm telling you, you're in shock. Snap out of it. You need to have something to eat and come back downstairs to help us figure this out. We've been banging our heads against a brick wall all day long—we need you."

I'm not sure where my head was at this point. I'm not sure why, after sitting in a chair all blessed day, I suddenly needed air. I think it was Bel's plea to help he and Arkady figure this out.

I think it was the idea I could somehow lead them to an answer like I'd done in the past, and the fear of failing them, of never having an answer, made me want to bolt. I always found the answer because of Win—we found it *together*.

Either way, I had to get away from the house, away from this life I'd created with Win.

I couldn't breathe from the need to get away. I don't understand why my will to go another round was so reluctant, but it grew in me like a festering infection. It strangled me like a tight shirt, and I had to break free.

Hopping off the chair, I pulled my robe off and ran to my closet to grab a jacket. I didn't care that I was still in my stinky pajamas. I didn't care that my hair looked as though I'd stuck my finger in a light socket—I needed to get away from this house.

"Stevie? What are you doing?"

Pulling on an old hoodie, I grabbed my phone and shoved it into the pocket. "I need to get out of this house, Bel. I need to do it *now*."

As I said those words, the desperate energy buried in me all day coiled then snapped, and I was all silent motion, running down the hall and taking the steps two at a time in order to get away.

I grabbed my car keys and threw the door open, the wind greeting me with its raw, drizzly chill.

"Steeevie!"

"I'll be back!" I yelled over my shoulder, the rain battering my face as I beeped my car open and hopped inside.

Drive. I just wanted to drive somewhere, anywhere but here, where my entire life, where the center of my universe, had crumbled to pieces.

As I backed out of the driveway and put the car in drive, I inhaled, feeling like I could truly breathe for the first time since this had begun.

And I did that. I drove aimlessly while the blur of the dark night whizzed past my car windows and my head, muddled and fuzzy, filled with disjointed thoughts of a life without Win. Filled with the sound of his voice, filled with the echo of his laughter.

I'm not sure where I went or how I finally came back to the house, or even when I arrived. I only know I was suddenly back in the driveway again, when dread welled in my belly.

A dread so real, so palpable, I wasn't sure I could get out of the car.

I dreaded going inside because Win wouldn't be there.

Win wouldn't be there...

Now the agony of hearing Win had left, without any proof he *hadn't* crossed over, socked me in the chest, making me want to curl up in bed and never leave. I've faced plenty of sadness in my life, plenty of disappointment, but this was different.

Bereft was the best word I could come up with to describe this merciless ache in my soul, and as I sat in my driveway, the driveway Win had designed himself, I almost couldn't move.

Leaning forward, I rested my forehead on the steering wheel and prayed this wretched emptiness, this feeling of abandonment would end. Numb had been so much better—so much easier.

All at once, I was very aware of everything around me, aware of every raw emotion I'd managed to tamp down today. The glow from the dashboard became too much, our favorite Pandora station, playing softly on the radio, became too loud. The lights from the house, dulled only by the pouring rain, hurt my head.

In that moment, the strains of "For Good" began to play in the car, the tinkling piano, the heart-wrenchingly beautiful voice of Kristin Chenoweth brought my agony bubbling to the surface...and that was the moment it all fell apart.

All my resolve, all my self-control slipped away, and anguish set in, clawing at my heart when she sang the words, *I've heard it said that people come into our lives for a reason...*

The tears I'd been too tired to cry or too determined to allow fell from my eyes in fat splotches, drenching my cheeks. I clung to the steering wheel, holding on with a tight grip as visions of the many adventures I'd shared with Win since we'd met rushed through my mind's eye.

Adventures we'd never again share—the life we'd built together, as unconventional as it was to any outsider, had been so wonderful. We'd managed to work around our deficits somehow. He'd given me so much more than money and a house with all the trimmings. He'd given me courage and strength. He'd given Bel and I a *home*.

He'd *given...*

How could I ever conceive of living without him?

As the last words of the song floated through the car—*Who can say if I've been changed for the better? But because I knew you, I have been changed for good*—I gasped for air, almost unable to breathe.

My ragged sobs tore through the interior of my tiny car—until a sharp rap at the window made me jump out of my skin, jolting me from of my tortured weeping.

I turned to find Dana's handsome face peering in at me, with Melba poking her head around his shoulder, an umbrella over their heads. But that handsome face went from smiling to grave concern as he popped open the door of the car.

"Stevie? Are you okay?" He held out his hand to me. "Here, let me help you." I must have recoiled, because he put a gentle hand on my shoulder. "It's okay, Stevie. It's just me, Officer Stick-Up-His-Butt, and Melba, too. You like us, I promise. We thought we'd drop by some food in case you needed it during your family emergency. C'mon. Let us help you inside."

I gave him my hand, but I stumbled when I tried to get out of the car, falling into him, likely from lack of sleep and food.

"Stevie? What's happening? *Please, please* tell me," Dana begged with an alarmed tone to his voice, gripping my shoulders as the wind tore at his normally perfect hair.

But how could I? How could I tell him the man I needed more than I've ever needed anyone in my life, the one person aside from Belfry who'd always been there for me, was gone, and I was just now feeling that loss?

Oh, and he wasn't just gone as in he left. He'd defected from the afterlife.

How could I explain that?

Looking up into his handsome face, so concerned, so not like the Dana I ran into at crime scenes, but the man who'd become my unwilling friend, I swallowed back another fresh batch of hysteria and reached out to him, grabbing his hand, willing the right words to come.

He held tight to me, squeezing my fingers. "Tell me, Stevie. Tell me what's going on. I've never, in all the time I've known you, *ever* seen you like this. So distraught…and you're scaring me. You're *really* scaring me. Talk to me. You can always, *always* talk to me. Please tell me you know that."

My chest throbbed and burned, tight with pain. "I… I lost someone very dear to me today. No one you knew, but someone who—" I gasped for air, clinging to his hand as tears began to slide down my face. "Someone who changed me. Someone who changed… who changed my life."

Dana stared at me, his eyes racing over my face. "Who, Stevie? How can I help? How can I ease your pain?"

Gulping the chilly night air, I shook my head and swiped at my cheeks, wiping my free hand on my jacket. "You can't. You can…can't," I rasped the word. Even words hurt. Everything hurt, but I somehow had to explain without telling him the truth. Instead, I called up a comparison, one I knew he could relate with. "Do you remember when you lost Sophia?"

Dana inhaled, his wide chest expanding with the effort. "I do. You were there for me, Stevie. You were always there when I needed you. Let me be here for you."

"Let me, too," Melba whispered, speaking for the first time since they'd arrived.

But I shook my head again, my heart tearing at the seams. "Do you remember how much that hurt, Dana? Do you remember it was as though someone stole the very breath from your lungs? Do you remember how blindsided you were?"

He didn't answer at first; instead, he pulled me into his strong embrace and pressed his cheek against the top of my head, while Melba placed a warm, supportive hand on my shoulder.

"Of course, Stevie. Of course, I remember."

"And do you remember how you just needed time to process her loss? How you needed to let it sit for a little while before you could face your friends and family?"

"Yes," he whispered into the night, a raw sound coming from his throat. "Yes."

"Let me do that, too, please?" I begged, choking out the words. "I promise…I promise I'll come to you when I'm ready. I-I promise."

"*Swear it*, Stevie. Swear it to both Melba and me, or I'm not leaving you here alone tonight. Not a chance."

I clenched my fist against his chest and pushed my knuckles into my mouth, both to keep from screaming and to allow me the time to speak the words he needed to hear so he would let me be in peace.

I didn't want to turn my friend away. I didn't want to hurt his feelings or shun his comfort, but I couldn't face anyone just yet. I couldn't explain…

"Stevie?" Melba said, her soft voice full of sympathy.

"*Yes*. Yes, I swear it to you."

I heard Melba inhale, felt her tug at my fingers, pull my hand into hers and rub my freezing-cold digits as the wind whipped at the umbrella and the rain pelted us.

I felt Dana sway, rocking me whether he knew he was or not, lulling me, soothing me. We stood there for a long time—or maybe it wasn't that long at all. I don't know. I didn't care. Right now, I didn't care where I was or what happened to me.

I just wanted Win. I wanted to hear his voice in my ear. I wanted him to taunt me about how horrible my taste in just about everything is. I wanted him to mock me about how I was slacking off with my workouts. I wanted to watch TV with him.

I wanted to hear him call me his dove one last time.

Just one last time.

As I said, I don't know how long we stood there in the cold night, the wind whistling through the trees Win had so carefully insisted we save when we'd remodeled the house and landscaped.

I only know, when Dana finally let me go, the fresh scent of his cologne and Melba's lasagna lingering in my nose, we were on the front porch. But I don't remember much else after stepping inside the house Win had so carefully, lovingly renovated, closing the door, and leaning back against the hard surface until my knees bent and I hit the ground with my backside.

And that's where I sat, Whiskey's head in my lap, the sound of deathly silence from above resonating in my ears.

It's where I fell utterly and completely apart for the second time.

CHAPTER 10

*A*s Bel sang "So This is Love" in my ear, I'm embarrassed to say this, but I had the mother of all meltdowns part two. My pendulum of emotions swung wildly from one extreme to the other, and I'm not proud of how I momentarily gave up, but I'm honest enough to admit I did.

When Bel began to sing, it reminded me that he used to croon that song to me when I was little. When I was all alone and afraid because my mother was off with her latest suitor.

He knew how much I loved the story of Cinderella, and he'd often joked he was the witch's version of the singing bluebirds from the movie. When I was a child, I often compared myself to the Disney princess. I didn't have an evil stepmother, but I had an absent one, a dismissive one who loved herself far more than she could ever love me.

At the end of her story, Cinderella had everything I

117

so desperately wanted. A home, love, a prince, acceptance. And okay, if I'm honest, a sweet pair of shoes.

As silly as it sounds, I didn't think about the anti-feminist take on it all and how her happiness was so keenly dependent upon a man sweeping her off her feet. I only thought about how much the prince loved her, and how much I wanted to be loved like that.

Now, as Belfry sang to me, I realized in my personal Cinderella story, Win was my prince. I don't mean in the traditional sense, either—not entirely. I don't need someone to sweep me off my feet and carry me off to the nearest castle, although he'd rather done that in the most avant-garde way.

But if he hadn't come along and given me this amazing experience with his money and this beautiful house, I would have rallied, because that's just what I do.

What I mean by that is this: he was my acceptance, my home, my true north, and losing him was unbearable. He was the first person to truly embrace who I am, and now, this empty space in my heart, this black void deep in my soul, whistled through me, proof of how much of him had become a part of me.

I didn't know how I'd survive without that. I know it's wrong, but I'm not sure I wanted to live in a world where there was no Win.

But there *was* no Win, and it appeared there would never be again, and right now, I needed to find a way, find an answer to how I'd ever get up off this floor, let alone move forward.

While I lost myself in my misery, while I steeped like a tea bag in pathetic sorrow, I didn't notice Belfry had stopped singing.

He rubbed his snout against my cheek, drying my endless tears. "Stevie B? C'mon, Boss. No more tears. Okay? Let's go make a pot of coffee and figure this out. That's what we always do. We figure this out. We *always* figure it out."

But there was nothing left to figure. We hadn't had a clue all day, and the clues we did have led to nothing. How could I possibly find someone who had literally disappeared from a place I couldn't see to investigate? A place where entry required my death?

Leaning my head back against the door, I inhaled a watery breath. "It's impossible, Bel. We have nothing. There is nothing. No amount of coffee or my laptop is going to figure this out. You heard what Arkady told us. The spirit said he crossed over."

"Well, guess what? I don't entirely believe that shizzle, okay? I think that's crapola, and you know it! Spirits are confused all the time. Maybe this one was confused, too. Until we know for sure Win's crossed over, we don't give up. We *never* give up."

I couldn't answer him. I had nothing to say. I only wanted to curl up in a protective ball, pull a blanket over my head and never come up for air.

"That's it. Get up, Stevie! Get up right now!" Belfry cried, using his nose to nudge my cheek in the most irritating way. "I won't have this. Not one second more! You've done all the wallowing you're going to do. We're

Cartwrights. Cartwrights don't wallow—we fight 'til the end."

"Yes, *malutka*, listen to tiny wing-ed creature, and get up. *Please*, my daffodil of love. I cannot bear to see you this way when there is nothing I can do to help. You must get up!" Arkady cried out. And I heard him.

I heard the desperate panic in his tone, I almost felt it grab hold of me and shake me, it was so rife. But it didn't motivate me to move.

Belfry buzzed at my face, swatting his leathery wings against my eyes. "Get up, Stevie Cartwright. You will get off your bum right now!"

No. No. No. Every bone in my body rebelled and ached, every muscle deflated and limp as a noodle. I couldn't get up. I never wanted to get up.

"Stop, Belfry. Stop. Please. No motivational speeches today. I can't. This isn't the part of the hockey game where we're down but not out and all we need is one hearty speech about working together as a team to make a comeback. I just can't!"

"You can and you will, young lady!" he ordered sharply. "When was the last time you gave up? When? *Never*. That's when. We came to this Podunk town with not much more than the clothes on our backs, and look where we are. Because you didn't give up, Stevie. You didn't give up, and you're not giving up today. Not today!"

Cue movie-like speech.

Still, I shook my head. No. No, I couldn't do it. I

couldn't face another single second of this world without Win with me. *I wouldn't.*

Belfry changed positions, hovering right in front of my face, his wings flapping furiously. "This is no different than any other mystery, and you're going to solve it. Figure out how, Stevie. Figure. It. Out."

As he demanded I do his bidding with incessant chatter, I grew angry. Irrational rage slithered along my spine and left my cheeks hot and red.

How dare he insist I figure this out when that's all I'd been doing all stinkin' week long, and it was tearing me to shreds, chewing me up from the inside!

"There is no mystery to solve, Belfry!" I spat the words, rage hitting me square in the gut for the first time. Rage for how I'd come to this place in my life.

I'd have never met Win if not because some vengeful, hideous warlock couldn't bear the idea I'd kept him from killing his own flesh and blood.

I was here because of Adam Westfield. All of this new pain was because of him. He was the reason I'd ended up in Eb Falls in the first place. He was the reason, and if I ever got my witch powers back again, I was going to nail him to the face of a mountain somewhere, but not before I turned his seething-with-hatred eyes black and blue.

But Bel wasn't going to give up. He raced back and forth in front of my swollen eyes. "Let's call Dita and your dad, Stevie. They'll help. They'll know what to do! You can't just take the word of one stupid spirit."

"We haven't had a clue in what? An entire day, Bel.

Not a legit one, anyway," I said, my words hollow. "*A full day*. I think the message was simple, Win decided to cross. That's what rebirth meant. Something moved him to go into the light. How can we fault him for that?"

"Then let's get your crazy parents here and have them ask around and make sure!"

I gave my head a violent shake, my knotted, mussed hair rubbing against the solid wood of the door. "I can't involve them, Bel. You know I can't. I can't risk them losing their powers, too. I won't."

"We need to find out the truth, Stevie! We can't just let this go. I know you're a hot mess of emotions right now. I know you're tired and overwrought with the fear of loss and you're raw, but what if the spirit is wrong! Silence from the other side means squat. Think. I need you to think about what we can do to find the truth!

Think. Hah! that's all I'd done since Win had disappeared. Think, think, think.

But that's exactly when a crazy, totally insane thought hit me.

Chalk it up to sleep deprivation or emotional imbalance, but…

"What if…?" I dragged myself off the floor, my body feeling as though it weighed as much as any healthy NFL player.

"What if what, *malutka*?"

A thread of energy lit a fire in my veins, making me stand up straight. "What if *I* tried to find the truth? Just me—no involvement from anyone from the coven or my parents?"

Bel's voice was disapproving, but I think deep down he knew what I meant. "Tried *how* exactly, Stevie?"

"What if I tried to summon Win? What if I tried some spells?"

∼

"This is battier than I am, Stevie!"

We'd moved to the living room where, despite every effort to convince Bel and Arkady otherwise, they thought I'd gone off the deep end. Listen, I know I was exhausted. I know I probably wasn't of sound mind, and for sure I wasn't of sound body, but what did we have to lose?

I began to pace the living room floor, tucking my hands into my damp hoodie. "What do we have to lose, Bel? What? My powers don't work and we go to plan B, right?"

"Stevie, you know what we have to lose!" he whisper-yelled as though the reason we shouldn't try was right here in the room with us. "If that crusty old battle-axe hears you fishin' around in the realms, she'll fly here on her broke-back broom faster'n you can say alacazam and eat you for breakfast. That's what!"

Oh, no. Nope, nope, nopety-nope.

I wasn't going to buy into the Baba Yaga scare. No way. She'd all but abandoned me and hadn't had thing one to do with me in ages. I wasn't going to let her stop me from finding out what happened to Win. She had no right to do anything with me, let alone interfere in any part of my life now that I was human.

Not one single right. Not even Satan was going to stop me from at least trying.

Still, feeling wildly contrary and maybe even a little spiteful, I countered with, "Well, how can she hear me if I'm not a witch, Bel?"

"She hears *everything*, Stevie. Those big ears of hers are everywhere!" he spat.

"*Malutka*, what is this you wish to do that upsets little marshmallow so much? Tell Arkady because he does not understand."

An eerie calm took over then, my rigid spine and tight muscles relaxed. Maybe it had to do with the fact that I was going to attempt to tap into my all but lost witch powers, something that once brought me a great deal of comfort, something that had come with great ease, something familiar.

Or maybe it was just that I knew they wouldn't work at all, but at least I was doing something instead of standing stock still, waiting for my life to further implode into a million more little pieces.

I don't know. Either way, I said, "I'm going to use a conjuring spell to try to summon Win."

"A *what*?"

"A *spell*, Arkady!" Belfry yelped in clear frustration with me. "A very hard to manage, not to mention dangerous spell! You know, *necromancy*? Bringing back someone from the dead? Keep up, would you, old man?"

"Like on that crazy television show *The Vampire Diaries?*" Arkady balked.

"Yeees!" Belfry yelped, flapping his wings with frantic swipes of the air.

"No, no, no! *Nyet!*" Arkady yelled. "You must not toy with such things, *malutka.* I cannot allow!"

Rubbing my grainy eyes, I stopped pacing and stared up at the ceiling of the living room, with its inlaid tile and glossy chandelier, and I exploded all over the joint.

"You cannot allow? *Allow?* How dare you tell me what you'll *allow?*" I roared in bone-weary anguish...in fear...in rage.

"Stevie!" Belfry yelled, zipping in front of my face, his wings still flapping furiously. "Look at me right now! You stop this insanity immediately. Understand? You will not talk to Arkady that way. He's as afraid as we are for Win. He spent all day with me while you got lost in your misery, trying to figure this mess out! He's our *friend,* Stevie. *Our friend.* I won't allow—yes, I said, *allow*—you to talk to him like that. Knock it the fudge off or I swear, I'll go dig up one of those nutbar witches we left behind in Texas and have them put a silencing spell on you so fast, your tongue'll fall out of your head. Knock. It. Off!"

It was then I blinked, my hand shaking as I covered my mouth in horror at my sharp words, and whispered between my fingers, "I'm sorry, Arkady. Oh...I'm so sorry."

"*Malutka,* please. Arkady begs you. Please sit down and take deep breath. You are tired. So tired. I see this on your beautiful face. Your eyes, they are red. Your legs, they are weary. Please, you must rest for little bit. Then we will think hard."

I made my way to the corner of the living room, reaching for the arm of the chair before I dropped down into it and leaned forward, gulping air like a fish out of water.

I was beginning to sound manic, and that was out of character for me—as out of character as giving up. I had to calmly explain my position, even if the momentary calm I'd felt moments ago was already long gone.

"I'm sorry, Arkady. I was wrong to speak to you that way, but we have to do something. *I* have to do something. *Please*, I need you to trust me. If I no longer have even a shred of my powers, none of it will matter anyway, but I have to try. Can't you two see that?" I sobbed hoarsely.

Out of the blue, I felt warmth surround my shoulders, and I almost called out Win's name, but it was a different aura than my International Man of Mystery's. It had a heavier feeling than Win's presence, less intimate somehow, yet equally soothing.

It was then I realized Arkady was hugging me, something he'd never done before, and I let him. I let him breathe calming words into my ear until that manic, clawing feeling pervading my body eased.

"There, there, my sweet honeydew. I was wrong to yell at you. I speak before I think. Arkady is afraid for you, *malutka*. That is all. We must do what you say is best—even if risk turn out to be greater than reward."

I almost chuckled at him using Win's words, but my misery wouldn't let me. "Thank you, Arkady. Thank you for trusting me. I promise you, I'll be careful. I really don't think it's going to make a hill of beans, but anything is better than sitting around waiting for something to happen."

"Wait one moment. You make hill of beans, too? How does beans help? Arkady does not understand," he replied as I felt his warmth leave my side and dissipate entirely.

Now I *did* laugh. "Just another stupid American expression." Pausing, I looked for Bel, who was pretty angry with me as it stood. "Belfry?"

"This is nutballs with more nutballs on top, Stevie."

Yes. This was nutballs, but I was willing to take that chance if it meant Win was still out there somewhere, and I refused to give in.

"Are you in or are you out?"

He buzzed back to my face, like some bizarre hummingbird/bat hybrid. "I'm telling you, if this works even a little, you're stewed. BY is going to make the remainder of your life a living hell, and she'll do it with her stupid leg warmers and neon hair scrunchies—"

"But—"

"But hold on!" Belfry cut me off. "And I'm saying this with great hesitation...your witch powers haven't worked in a long time. You haven't even had a small blip lately. Now, I'm just going to say one thing, and then I won't say it again. Be prepared for that old hag just in case, because I'm just as stressed about a missing Win as you are, and if I snap with Baba, I can still go down for my crimes. I'll end up in witch prison as a lifer, and you'll be here with a hundred cats to fill the hole in your heart left behind by your failed necromancy."

Bel always helped me see the other side of things, and I hadn't thought about his involvement. "Then I won't do it. I won't risk your safety."

"Yes. Yes, you will. She can't put me in jail if I don't slug her in that smug sourpuss of hers. I think I can promise not to slug her."

"Are you sure?" I asked hesitantly.

"I'm sure. Now forget me, what spell shall we start with?"

"Conjuring?"

"It's as good as any," he answered.

"Whoa. Explain conjuring to Arkady, please. So I know what we face."

"Our girl here's gonna try and raise the dead, buddy. Hold on to your *ushanka*. It's about to get real in here if she can pull this off."

"Please be careful, *malutka*. I do not wish to lose you, too. You are my friend. I love you. We are family."

"I love you, too, Arkady," I whispered upward, my heart full, but also determined.

Holding my breath, I closed my eyes and tried to

recall from memory the conjuring spell, knowing it was a foolish attempt, a desperate effort to locate Win.

But I almost didn't care. I'd had blips in my powers before, hadn't I? Small blips, certainly not a blip as large as a conjuring spell, but anything was worth trying.

Bel fluttered nervously about the room, but his support was clear when he asked, "Stevie? Do you remember it without the book?"

The book. That stupid, stupid book of spells the coven had treated as though it were a Bible. The book we'd coveted, protected…and for what? So it could all be taken from me?

So when the time came, and I needed my coven most, when I needed my powers the most, I could fumble around foolishly, almost delirious from lack of sleep, without the book I'd have protected with my own life?

Right now, I despised everything witch. All of it. Because I needed that book and my coven sisters now more than ever. I needed just a little bit of magic from someone—anyone—to help locate Win, and I'd never felt more alone since being shunned than I did right now.

Still, I remembered. I remembered every stinkin' word.

So I nodded, forcing my breathing to steady itself so Belfry wouldn't panic and fear for my sanity, squeezing my eyes shut so my threatening teardrops wouldn't fall.

Running my tongue over my dry lips, I said, "I remember. Say it with me, okay, Bel?"

He pushed himself tighter against my neck. "Always, Stevie. *Always*. Ready?"

Clenching my hands together, I began, "Ashes to ashes, dust to dust. Come to me now, into this realm you must."

"With conviction, Stevie," Bel whispered-yelled. "Say it again."

For someone who'd been against this, he sure was fierce now.

So I repeated, closing my eyes, focusing every cell of my energy on making Win appear. "Ashes to ashes, dust to dust. Come to me now, into this realm you must! Ashes to ashes, dust to dust. Come to me now, into this realm you must! Ashes to ashes, dust to dust. Come to me now, into this realm *you must!*"

CHAPTER 11

I waited then. I waited and prayed to any entity willing to listen that Win would appear and we'd figure everything out from there. No matter what body he was in, no matter what condition he was in, we'd figure it out.

But nothing happened.

The four corners of the living room were as quiet as they'd been when I'd convinced myself this was a good idea. In fact, if my spell were accompanied by a sound affect, it would be the one you hear when your character's on empty.

My shoulders slumped as the dark claws of depression sank their talons into my psyche, reminding me I wasn't a witch anymore.

If I'd even had a shred of hope as a witch of conjuring up a soul—and mind you, it's very dangerous, necromancy is—it was small. But as an ex-witch who hasn't had her powers in over two years? Probably not a chance in Hades.

"No, no, no, my enchilada. You must not give up!" Arkady cried, his voice thick with emotion. "Try something else. You have not used your powers in long time. Maybe this is wrong spell. Maybe you rusty. Try another!"

Belfry chirped his agreement, injecting enthusiasm into his words. "Maybe he's right, Stevie! Let's try another one. Try them all. Every bloody last one!"

My how the tides had turned. I felt as though they were both humoring me, egging me on with the realization this wasn't going to work, and if it calmed me down, if it gave me purpose, they were all for it, because it couldn't hurt anyone anyway.

Struggling with this sudden helpless, dark feeling, I shuddered a breath as fear took root in my belly before a smidge of sanity returned. "We're not supposed to use our spells for personal gain…" I muttered, as though I hadn't known that from the start.

"Well, if you're not a witch, if your powers are really still kaputski, what difference will it make?" Belfry shot my words back at me. "Just try. We have to try everything we can!"

Hearing Bel's voice, as agonizingly desperate as Arkady's, for the first time since this began, I realized how selfish it was of me to believe I was the only one who loved Win. They loved him, too. He was family to all of us, and if I didn't at least give it my best effort, how could I live with myself?

Running a hand through my disheveled hair, I flexed my fingers and used my shoulder to wipe my eyes free of pending tears. "Okay… Oh! I know, let's try a time-traveling spell, right, Bel? Remember it?"

He chuckled. "Remember it? Are you kidding? Do you remember what happened when Orwell Hanson recited one by mistake because he forgot to put his glasses on and ended up back in a cave with a bunch of cavemen? How could I forget?"

The corner of my mouth lifted in a smirk of a smile. "I'll give you that. It was definitely funny to see Orwell in a bearskin rug with a spear he'd made with his little Neanderthal friends."

"So are we gonna sit around and rehash memories about it or are we gonna do this, Stevie?" Bel encouraged.

My heart pumped erratically, but in for a penny, in for a pound. "We're gonna *do this*." I prayed we would do this.

"That's the spirit!" Arkady encouraged.

"Just make sure you picture the time period in your mind, Stevie. Be very clear, understood?

I nodded, my hands clammy, my legs weak. Breathing in, I focused every cell of my body, every ounce of the little energy I had left and began the incantation. "Hands of the clock, take me back, return to yesterday. Take me back so I might stay!"

∽

*a*n hour later, we'd tried every frickin'-frackin' spell in the book, or the ones I could remember by heart, anyway, and had come up with absolutely nothing. If my composure was gone, my sanity had left with it, and I was cracking once more.

The funny thing about cracking is, you know you're doing it, but you can't seem to stop the forward motion, you can't pull up on the reins because all the self-control you've so carefully utilized no longer matters to you.

You don't care that you're about to lose control and crack. You don't care about your dignity or how you appear to other people. You don't care about pretty much anything. You just want to let go and let the cracking happen.

And I did exactly that. Boy oh boy, did I ever do that, and I remember the very moment I let it all hang out. I remember when my field of giving the letter Fs dried up, and I'm not even going to ask you to pardon my French because at that moment, I didn't want a pardon. I only wanted the agony of losing Win to end.

Anyway, as I said, I know when I cracked completely. It was when I heard Bel's voice quiver for the first time since this had begun—I heard him really waver.

"I don't know what to do, Stevie," he said on a deep shudder, his voice steeped in defeat. "I...I don't know how to guide you through this..."

If Bel was nothing else, he was my familiar first.

He's not just an adorable little ball of marshmallowy cotton with a squeaky voice and tiny wings. He's my moral compass, my eyes, my ears, my confidant since childhood. That he was as beaten as I, left me feeling helpless.

But only for a moment before I decided, as long as I was cracking, I might as well crack big.

Really big.

Whirling around, I tightened my damp, smelly hoody around my waist and looked up at the ceiling, widening my stance so I wouldn't tip over, bracing myself.

And then I wound up for the out-of-control pitch I was about to make. "Baba Yaga!" I screamed with such ferocity, my throat burned. "Get your eighties-loving, weirdo-shoulder-pad-wearing, crotchety old backside here *nooow!*"

"Stevie? Have you lost your bloody marbles?" Belfry yelled, flitting about the room in a frantic circle. "She's going to flay us alive!"

"Then hide, Belfry. Hide now, because we have no hope! There's nothing left to help us find Win but her and her magic. No stone unturned, right?" I sobbed. *"No stone unturned."*

I don't know if I always knew or if I even believed Baba could still hear me, now that I was no longer a witch, but maybe I had a feeling deep down that she'd kept tabs on me since I'd been booted from the coven.

Maybe to monitor whether I was trying to find a way to retrieve my powers, or maybe even just because at one time, I'd meant something to the coven —to her.

I told myself on many occasions I didn't care. She'd done her job. I can't fault her there, I suppose. Sometimes your imperious leader has to make choices that aren't always favorable but for the greater good.

Though, I can't say how leaving me high and dry after I'd shown compassion to the small child of a monster was the greater good, but whatever. I broke a rule, and she made me pay. End of story.

Still, Baba was a decent being. She ruled with an iron fist, but she had a heart, and it was that heart that left me wondering if she still listened for me, in spite of the coven rules.

But in the process of cracking, I no longer cared if she listened because she fretted over me, and I didn't care about the consequences of calling her out. Baba was a conduit. She, or someone she knew, could tell me what had happened to Win. That was *all* I cared about.

I was at straw-that-broke-the-camel's-back stage of the game. I had nothing left to lose and more determination than good sense.

Closing my eyes, I inhaled deeply and screamed, "Baaaba Yaaaga! I, Stephania Cartwright, summon thee to this realm—*now*!"

When she appeared before me, in all her '80s regalia, the scent of Love's Baby Soft in the air, her signature green smoke fanning out behind her, I found out, apparently, she *did* still hear me.

Her beautiful eyes met mine for the first time in a

long time—and they weren't the kind that said, "Hey, kid. How ya been?"

No. In fact, they were flashing and intense, but remember, I'd lost all self-control at this point, and I didn't care how I was received by the great and powerful BY.

I only cared that she give me what I wanted, and I wanted to know where Win was before it was too late. I couldn't let it be too late, and if it was too late, I needed to know he'd had safe passage.

"Stephania, as you well know by coven law, after a shunning, you're not supposed to contact me," she said, her voice stern as she fluffed her Madonna-like skirt and smoothed her bi-level hair back from her ever-youthful face.

The neon bangle bracelets she wore clanked when she crossed her arms under her breasts and stared me down.

I don't know if you recall, but Baba is a lover of all things '80s—clothes, music, hair. Her outfits were outrageous, despite the fact that she was gorgeous in them.

"I know," I seethed, lifting my chin to stare defiantly at her. I think when you go kaplooey the way I did, you go through several stages leading up to total bananapants, and this was the angry-with-the-world-right-before-the-total-bananapants stage. "And I don't give a witches broom. I need your help, and I need it *now*. No. I take that back. I *demand* it now!"

"*Stevie!*" both Arkady and Bel admonished in unison.

I stomped my foot (yep, you read that right), tightening my jaw. "Don't you *Stevie* me, you two! Don't you dare! I'm at my wit's end. I can't take anymore! I can't bear the idea that we don't know for sure if Win's really gone. I want confirmation, and I want it now!"

Baba circled me, eyeballing me with eyes of fire and a mouth that thinned until it almost disappeared. "How dare you ask that of me, Stephania," she said, her tone cool with inconvenience.

So here's the part where, I if I hadn't lost it before, I totally lost my shiznit. Lost it in ten different ways.

"*How dare I?* How dare I ask you for something?" I bellowed, making her crazy hair blow upward from the force of my screech. "How dare you take *everything* I've ever loved away from me without a single word! How dare you leave me stranded as though I never existed! Well, look at me now, Baba!" I spread my arms wide to encompass the room. "I sure bounced back, didn't I? And I'm not going to let *anyone* take my life again. You *owe* me, and I think somewhere in that cold, black heart of yours, you know you do. *You know it!*"

"Stevie!" Belfry cried as Whiskey, my little traitor, rubbed his head against Baba's leg, looking for love. "Stop! Stop right now!"

Baba reached down and ran a slender hand over Whiskey's head, her eyes zeroing in on my familiar. "Belfry? How is it you've lost control of your witch?"

"*His witch?*" I roared, clenching my fists to keep

from clocking her in the nose. "I'm not a witch anymore, thanks to you, or this little summoning wouldn't be happening at all! I'd have located Win all on my own!"

Almost immediately, Baba's eyes softened and her head cocked in curiosity. "You mean the delicious British fellow? That Win?"

Baba had paid me a visit a while back, and she'd met Win, who she'd fawned over and been utterly delightful to, and at the time, it made me want to hack up my lunch. But that she remembered him gave her a frame of reference.

I needed her to have a frame of reference, to understand this was no small request on my part. I wasn't asking her to save just anyone because I'm an empathetic fool and love a happy ending. This was Win.

I simmered down, but only enough to say, "Yes. That's the one."

Smiling absently as though she were recalling a happy memory, she gazed at me. "And what's happened to your Win, Stephania?"

My lips thinned while ugly thoughts of holding her down and forcing her to help me raced through my head. "I don't know, but I need your help to find out. I just want to know he's safe. I need to know if he went to the other side."

She gave me a blank look, the one that said I had a lot of nerve, her unlined face passive. "And how do you propose I do that?"

I openly gaped at her, my anger returning, my

stomach rolling. "You know *exactly* how to do that, Baba. There's a rumor going around in the afterlife that he's crossed. I need to know for certain if that's true."

She stared at me some more, her gorgeous eyes scanning me from head to toe. "I assume he's been with you since my last visit? All this time, Stephania? You've grown close?"

Tucking my arms under my breasts, I suddenly felt self-conscious. Even in '80s garb, Baba was beautiful, and I looked like a roughed-up, greasy, unwashed hag. "We have…" I muttered, my eyes falling to the floor, my bravado faltering.

"Isn't crossing into the light what one does when they make a choice to leave their appointed plane?"

"You know that's what happens. But let me explain. Please listen to me, and you'll understand why I summoned you."

So I explained, in the best way I knew how, and as she listened to me, her perfect face never moving an inch, I calmed a bit.

And I told her everything, complete honesty. I told her my fear that he'd decided to plane hop and possibly body surf, something I know she wholly disapproved of. I told her about the strange messages we didn't understand. I told her what Arkady had heard.

All of it.

When I was done, she lifted a hand to brush the hair from my face, but she shook her head. "You know if I locate him, that would be using magic for personal gain, Stephania, don't you? It's not allowed."

Instantly, my anxiety, ugly and thick, bubbled to the surface again. I batted her intrusive hand from my face, my breaths coming in choppy pants as my one last hope began to fade.

"*Please*! I'm begging you, Baba Yaga."

She reached out again, her face muted in sympathy. "Sweet girl—"

"Please!" I cried, pushing her away.

"Stephania," she began, but I wasn't letting her get away so easily.

Fear and hopelessness began to ratchet up, notch after notch, clawing at me as I burst at the seams. "Please, please don't take this one thing away from me! Everything has been taken away! *Everything!* Do you hear me? I lost everything when you sent me away!" I screamed, the pressure in my chest, the merciless headache pounding in my temples, all lent to this desperation I couldn't contain.

I couldn't bottle it up anymore.

Baba looked at me, her sharp eyes scanning my face. "Stephania—"

"*No!*" I belted out the word, so loud, the pictures on the wall rattled as I shook my head back and forth, a river of tears coursing down my face. "No, no, *no*! I rebuilt my life, and I did that all by myself when you shipped me off as though I were some dirty secret you had to hide, and then Win found me. He *saved* me! *He* did that! He gave me everything, everything I have today. We did this together, as a team. We're a team," I sobbed hoarsely, so distraught, I almost doubled over.

"Stevie," Bel soothed in my ear. "Please. Now *I'm* begging you. Please calm down. This can't be good for you. Please, please, sweet girl."

I know my eyes were wild. I know my movements were shaky and disjointed. I know I looked like a stark-raving lunatic. But I still didn't care. I didn't give a wit about how I looked or sounded. I just wanted to know where Win was. I wanted Win back. However I could have him, I *needed* Win, and I would not be turned away.

I began to pace, feeling the frantic rise and fall of my breathing making me dizzy, but I couldn't stop. If I stopped, I didn't know if I could ever move again.

"*Malutka*, my beautiful, kind *malutka*, I cannot bear this. I cannot bear your suffering. I, too, beg you. Please. Please, you must stop," he whispered. "Belfry is right. This is not good for you. You will make yourself sick."

"I don't care, Arkady! Don't you see, I don't care! What's not good for me is being without Win! Without all of us—*together*. You, me, Belfry, Whiskey, Strike and *Win*. I won't do it. I won't lose him and this life we've created if he didn't cross over! Do you hear me? So I'll do whatever you want, whatever you say— but don't you dare tell me no, Baba Yaga!" I sneered at her, shaking a finger under her nose as tears raced down my cheeks. "Don't you dare let everything be taken from me *again*! I don't want to hear that magic isn't for personal gain. I never, ever once used my magic for anything but what it was intended, and still you took it all away! I *personally gained* nothing from this gig!"

"*Malutka—*"

But I whipped a hand upward to silence him, my breathing ragged. "Now, I don't care about your stupid rules. I don't care what the council says. *I. Don't. Care!* I know you can tell me where he is, and if he's safe. I know you can find him with a location spell. It's a simple spell. Tell me where he is, Baba, and I'll take care of the rest. I'll never ask you for a single thing again if you tell me where Win is!"

In my frantic pacing, I tripped over my exhausted feet and fell, crumpled as though I were boneless, my pajamas, dirty from the rain, twisting around my legs, but when Baba reached out to help me up, I rose to my knees and grabbed her wrist.

And as my tears fell, I whispered raggedly, "Please. I just need to know if he's okay. If he's safe. If it means he crossed into the light…I'll accept that as our fate, but I need to know!"

Baba knelt down next to me, lifting my chin with one hand while latching onto the hand I used to hold her wrist, anchoring me. Her strength real, flowing through me like a warm balm.

"You're the most selfless being I know, Stephania," she said softly, hauling me upward and setting me from her. "Only *you* would ask that this lovely man's well-being come before yours. That you would let him go, if that's what made him happy, only enforces my instincts about you. You're all the things everyone should aspire

to be. The coven misses you. *I* miss you. But for now…
because it has to be this way, because you can't come
back, I want to give this to you. Because you're right—
you're owed a debt."

"Give this to me?" I didn't understand. Were we on
to find Win or not? "I don't understand…"

But she didn't answer me directly. "Belfry!" she
called, snapping her fingers and pointing to my shoulder, indicating he should land there. "Take care of our
girl, would you please? She'll need you now more
than ever."

Almost the second she spoke so cryptically, Baba
snapped her fingers again—and our living room was
no more.

Everything tilted, went about as sideways as it gets
before it righted itself.

"Stevie?" Bel whispered. "Where are we?"

"*Malutka?* What is this?"

As our surroundings became clearer, as the fuzzy
outlines of our location sharpened, I blinked as I began
to understand.

"A hospital. We're in the ICU unit of a hospital."

CHAPTER 12

I stood rooted to the white floor, still in my stinky pajamas with my hoodie tied around my waist, and fuzzy slippers on my feet, giving the quiet corridor a good once-over.

There was a long stretch of pale green hallway, dimly lit for the evening. Some hushed conversation down the hall somewhere was happening, but for the most part, it was quiet. Machines beeped and hissed, and there was a light glow in each of the rooms from heart monitors.

Hospital. We were definitely in the hospital. But where? It sure didn't look like Eb Falls General. I'd been to the hospital several times since I'd moved back, and it didn't look like this at all. The halls were wider, the windows both wider and taller. When I looked out at a row of them, spanning the right wall, all I saw was lights from a city. But it certainly wasn't Eb Falls, or even Seattle.

Bel tucked himself against my ear as I oriented myself. "I don't get what just happened or where we are, Boss."

Noting a sign for a bathroom just ahead of us, on quick feet, I made a break for it and ducked inside, locking the door. I headed for the mirror, my state of undress sinking in as I shook my head. "I don't get it, either."

Bel hopped to the pristine white sink and looked up at me. "Okay, so BY, that crusty old hen, said she owed you. In the history of witches, I've never heard that phrase uttered. I don't know why she suddenly decided she owed you, but whatever. She said she wanted to give this to you. What exactly is *this?*"

My head spun as I flipped on the cold-water tap and ran my fingers under the faucet to splash some water on my stinging, swollen eyes. "Well, this means one of two things. Either Win is here...or she screwed up royally and dumped us on the wrong floor and we're really supposed to be in the psyche ward."

"*Malutka*, listen to Arkady. I see how she look at you, your Baba Yaga. She does not do this with malice. Her heart is pure. She do something nice. This is something nice."

Belfry snorted. "I'm not even going to get into the purity of BY, but wow, Stevie B... Way to give our former leader some H-E-double-hockey-sticks. You really went for it, kiddo."

The magnitude of what I'd done, what I'd said, hit

me then. When I was in the middle of reaming BY a new one, when I was begging and scraping, I never once stopped to think about how far I'd gone because for the thousandth time, I didn't care. I had nothing to lose.

Now, looking at my reflection, wild-eyed and greasy-haired, gave me pause. Big, big pause. "I feel like I'm going to pay for that somewhere down the road. But I didn't care. I guess I *still* don't care. But I sort of lost it, and I'm sorry you guys had to see that."

"Oh, you lose it all right. You lose it *big*. But it is okey-doke. You were tiger, *malutka*. You give me great pride feeling in my chest."

My cheeks went hot red. "I know. I know. But sometimes the reward is greater than the risk."

We all snickered together but then I sobered. "So BY's reasons for granting me this aside...we're here. She didn't do this without reason. She sent us here, to an ICU unit. BY doesn't make mistakes. So, we need to figure out precisely what this means. We need a plan, guys."

"Oh, thank goddess you're talking plans, Boss. Thought I'd lost ya there."

I thought he had, too. "Not a chance."

"Okay, Arkady ready for plan. Let us make plan."

As I splashed my face again and dried my hands, I pondered. "So, the obvious answer to why we're here is, Win's here somewhere, too. The answer to why Win's here is also obvious. He's successfully body hopped into a dying body. Do we agree?"

"He would have to have a body to be in place such as this, Stevie. Arkady agree."

You'd think hearing that would thrill me to my marrow, but the truth was, it frightened the life out of me. If Win really was here and in a host body, one that wasn't too damaged, he might not remember who we were. I prayed he'd remembered that he could lose everything he was seeking when he went into this crazy mission. Like his memory of us. The memory of his life's work, the house, our adventures, *everything*.

"Oh, Stevie," Bel said on a long breath, and I knew he was thinking exactly what I'd been thinking.

"Family!" Arkady said sharply, clapping his hands. "I know what you think, but we must not think bad thoughts. We must do first things first. We must see if Win is even here, yes? Otherwise, this is all for naught, and we need to find new path."

Gripping the edge of the sink, I let my head hang between my shoulders. "You're right, Arkady. Thank you for keeping me from going off the deep end again. So yes, a little recon is necessary." I paused and stopped obsessing over the why's and where's and focused on the task. "Arkady, you scope the floor. Look in each room and see if you can find him."

"But wait," Belfry said, his voice distant as I'm sure he, too, pondered the million-and-one scenarios. "How will we know it's Win? Arkady can look all he wants, but how the heck will we even know it's him if he's in someone else's body, and doesn't remember us, and we no longer know what he looks like?"

Dang. Foiled again. But… "BY wouldn't drop us here out of the ether if he wasn't somewhere in this hospital. That has to be why we're here. So we go with that until we can't. As to knowing which body he's in, I suggest looking at the most critical cases. If he body surfed, he'd need a host that's on its way…er, out."

I cringed saying those words. I hated that a death would be involved, no matter how you sliced it, but that was the simple truth of the matter, and I was going to trust Win would pick the right body to do something this outlandish.

"Okey-doke. I go look."

"Hey, Arkady? Find out where the heck we are, too, would you? We're not in Eb Falls, for sure."

"*Dah*. You stay here with fluffybutt. Arkady be right back."

I sat down on the toilet and rested my shaking legs. My heart steadily beating a harsh pitter-pat. We were close. I knew we were close. That gut feeling sat stubbornly in the pit of my stomach.

"You okay, Boss?"

Looking down at my pajamas, the spatter of coffee across the front, the dirty cuffs at my ankles, I groaned. "I'm a little bit of a wreck. I look like I just rolled out of a night spent in a Dumpster after a drunken bender."

"You'll get no argument from me," he quipped in a light tone, landing on my head to fuss with my hair. "So tell me your fears, Boss. I know you have 'em, because I do, too."

"What if Win doesn't remember us, Bel? Have we

149

really talked about the repercussions? How do you feel about that?"

He stopped moving and hopped to my shoulder. "Here's what happens. If he stuck to his body-surfing code, the host body will have no one. No one to turn to, and he'll be confused and afraid. He'll need someone. *We're* his someone, Stevie. We'll always be his someone. He's family—forever. So we do what we do. We take his broke-back butt home, fix him up, and make him love us all over again whether he likes it or not."

My heart swelled with Bel's loyalty, with his dedication to me—to Win.

I held out my hand for Bel to jump into my palm and brought his nose to my lips, dropping a kiss on his snout. "I love you, Belfry. You're the best friend any witch or otherwise could have."

"*Malutka?*"

I held my breath and closed my eyes. "Did you find him?"

There was a very long pause, an uncomfortable, nerve-wracking pause, and then he said, "Yes. I think I find Zero."

~

"*H*e's in his *brother's* body? In Balthazar's?" I murmured in wonder. "Balthazar's dying?"

Yet, that explained the crazy message on my bathroom mirror. *Look 4 bath.* That had to mean "look for

Balthazar," and somehow the message had become twisted...but that also meant the message had to have been from Win.

Excitement and fear danced together in a tangle of emotions as I fought to keep focused. Getting to Win was priority one, before any of the other worries could be attacked.

Arkady sounded shaken up when he spoke. The slight tremor to his voice, one he'd never admit, was unmistakable. "*Dah*, Stevie. I see Balthazar's name on chart. He is in coma on life support here at Chicago General."

"Were in *Chicago?*" I breathed in. "Deep-dish pizza. Of course!"

"That Winterbutt. So clever," Bel praised.

I bit the inside of my cheek. "And why is he here? Did you see?"

"He come to hospital with fractured skull. He look so much like Win, Stevie. It shock Arkady speechless. They are *exactly* the same. His room is right down hall. You can see for yourself."

Bel whistled his approval. "Holy Winterbutt! He did it—yippee! I knew he could do it!"

Now I began to shake, an uncontrollable, violent shake that spread over my body like wildfire. Win... Win might already be here. Just feet away. I'd be able to touch him, see him instead of only imagining him.

But, whoa Nellie. There was a caveat to this mess. "How do we know he's actually in Balthazar's body?"

"Booo for technicalities," Belfry said.

"You know I'm right, Bel. So, Win's twin brother is in a room, in a coma on life support, with a fractured skull. How do we know he made it into Balthazar's body? He'd had to have died and been brought back for Win to slip in. Maybe the host body didn't die yet, and Win's hovering on some plane, waiting for his chance to get into his brother's body. Maybe that's still Balthazar in there."

"Ah, but it would account for long silence since almost two days, *malutka*. Maybe he jump into body, and that is why he is so quiet." Then he laughed, a hearty, cheerful rumble. "My Zero! I think he do it! Hurrah for Zero!"

Stuffing my knuckle in my mouth, I winced. "I hate to be the pin in your bromance bubble, Arkady, but we need to know for sure if he's in there. If he's in a coma, there's no way to know. He can't tell us because, well, *he's in a coma.*"

"There sort of is," Bel offered, hopping off me and back onto the sink. "We could just ask the nurses if Balthazar coded at any point, right? If he coded, Win probably took the opportunity to jump in when it happened."

"Oh, good point, Bel!" I almost reached for the door handle, but my appearance stopped me. "Well, we *could* ask—if I didn't look like I've just come back from an all-nighter. And besides that, they're not going to tell me anyway. I'm not family, and if he's been here in a coma for any length of time, they know he doesn't have any. Those were Win's rules of engagement, right? No ties to anyone? Balthazar was a foster kid and a vagabond—a mean one at that. Last I knew, he was working in a cell phone store. There are probably very few people who've visited him, if any at all. So how do we find out?"

"You could pretend to be a long-lost relative, maybe a girlfriend? It's not like you don't know how to pretend, Stevie. You do it all the time when we investigate a crime."

I held out my dirty pajama shirt. "Looking like this? What I need is a disguise."

But Baba had teleported us here. I had no money, no clothes, no phone. I didn't want to look a gift horse in the mouth, but we were virtually stranded.

"*Malutka*! Listen to Arkady. I have big-big idea…"

~

*A*djusting my surgical mask as I approached the ICU unit's desk, I was grateful it hid a multitude of the sins of the past few days. I looked like you-know-what, and I knew it, but my red, swollen eyes lent to the tired temp-nurse role I was about to play.

Arkady's suggestion to dress up as a surgical nurse was brilliant. Finding scrubs, a mask and a cart had been the easiest parts of this—especially so late at night. The rest was going to be tricky at best if I got caught.

I wasn't exactly winning awards for my acting, but

as I came closer to the ICU desk, with two nurses attending, I reminded myself this one was for Win.

I purposely didn't look into the window of the room Win was in, keeping my face averted to the glass, or I felt certain I'd falter. I needed to keep it together, and seeing him for the first time, live and in person, wasn't meant to be done without preparation.

Bel hid in the pocket of my hoodie, which I'd turned inside out and rewrapped around my waist to keep him close.

"Go get 'em, tiger," he whispered, just seconds before I stopped short at Win's room, praying I could get in there without being seen.

Thankfully, his room was positioned far enough away from the desk that, if the nurses turned their back for just a second, I could slip in unnoticed.

We'd decided to see if I could read Balthazar's chart before we went chatting up nurses and I'd be forced to play a more vocal part. I tend to ramble when I'm lying, and I know as much about medical procedures as your average *Grey's Anatomy* watcher. I couldn't risk being caught.

"Stevie! Go now, popsicle!" Arkady whispered to me, and I paid heed, slipping inside the room and letting the door close with a hush.

He'd promised to give me the outline of the room so I wouldn't be tempted to peek at Win as a just in case a nurse showed up and I had to hide.

Scrunching my eyes shut, I whispered upward, "Gimme the lay of the land, Arkady so I won't crash into anything if I have to make a break for a hiding place."

"Two beds. Zero to the left, old man to right. Both on life support. Window in middle of room. Chair in right corner. Two nightstands. One on right of old man's bed, one on left for Zero. Many, many machines."

As I opened my eyes, I assessed and familiarized myself with the room only in my direct line of vision, eerily lit with red and green lights from the heart and vitals monitors.

You didn't have to be a witch to know death waited here. I felt it wrap around me, oppressive and heavy, as I listened to the alternate beeps and tweets sounding off their readings.

I swallowed hard and clenched my hands around the handle of the cart, forcing myself to keep my eyes glued to anything but the body in the bed to my left.

"Belfry, close the curtains. We can't attract attention."

Bel wiggled out of my pocket and zipped upward, moving out of my line of vision, but I heard as he pulled the curtain to the window shut.

Feeling a smidge safer we wouldn't be spotted, I asked. "What if I just take a peek? Just a little one."

"*Nyet!*" Arkady barked the prickly order. "Do not look at Zero, *malutka*," Arkady warned. "I must insist you do not lose head at the sight of him. You are too emotionally charged up to resist pausing to really see him for first time. Every second counts if you do not wish to be caught. Read chart first. It is at end of bed. Stay focused, sweet one."

Arkady was right. I couldn't promise I wouldn't get caught up in the moment and forget all about why I was here because I was enamored with actually being able to see him. Goodness knows, my emotions had gotten the better of me plenty during this mess.

Keeping my eyes down, I paid particular attention to the white knit blanket and the edge of the bed. Locating the chart, I grabbed it up and flipped it open, forcing my crazy curiosity and excitement to sit and stay—if only for a few minutes more.

"Are you kidding me?" I hissed as my eyes scanned a series of scribbly words and half sentences. "Who could read this? It's like Greek. I can't tell if he's in a coma or he's had breast implants."

"Hold up chart, *malutka*. Let Arkady see."

I did as I was told, all the while fighting the impulse to look at Win. In fact, I turned my back to his bed and focused my gaze on the man across from him.

An elderly gentleman with snowy-white hair, a frail frame, and a million machines hooked up to his body. The drip, drip, drip of the IV mesmerized me, the pumping up and down of his chest, the long tubes wheezing in his throat.

As Arkady read Balthazar's chart, my heart hurt for whoever he was, clearly critical, and incredibly frail.

"Sweet cabbage, *malutka*. Arkady cannot read, either, and I know how to read many languages. Is mess," he said, interrupting my thoughts.

"So now what?" I asked, my hands dropping to my sides while I used every ounce of will I had to keep from turning around. "Do I go play nurse? Do you think I can pull it off?"

But I didn't have to worry about playing anything…

"Awww, hey…Winterbottom, is it? Super-spy extra-ordinaire? Look who came to our body-surfing party? It's your ladylove. Stevie! It's wonderful to see you," a playful voice growled from the door.

My heart began to pump so hard, my ears hurt from the pound and my hands went icy cold. I looked up and to the door at my right to find a short, balding man in a lab coat slipping inside the room.

So, here's the thing. I pretty much knew who it was, but I think it goes without saying, in times of pure terror, we do stupid stuff. We go into the basement when everyone is screaming for us to go the other way. We take the flight we dreamt had crashed the night before we boarded.

We ask lame questions like the one I asked when I already knew the answer. *"Who are you?"*

"That really is stupid questions, don't you think?" he asked as he began to disrobe, throwing his lab coat on the floor at the foot of Win's bed.

Okay, I'd give him that. It was stupid.

Oh, and the "him" in the equation being Adam Westfield. Using, according to the nametag, a Dr. Marrakesh's body.

My pulse thrashed in my ears like a whale out of water, but I reminded myself that he was in a human body, something he appeared to possess with great ease. I wondered vaguely if that had something to do with him being a warlock.

The question was, could he use his magic while in this particular human body? I couldn't remember if he'd used magic when he'd possessed poor Edmund, the teen who'd worked for our local caterer, Petula. I was so drunk from lack of sleep, I couldn't remember since the last time we'd run into each other. But my hope was, at the very least, his magic was dulled.

So I took a chance and postured, maybe foolishly, but I did it anyway by walking right up to him and jamming my face in front of his. Show no fear.

Before crossing my arms over my chest, I yanked the surgical mask off and narrowed my gaze. "I think the question is, what are you doing here, *Adam*?"

He cocked his shiny head and grinned—and it was when he smiled from ear to ear, when his round face and moon-shaped cheeks lifted, that he epitomized evil.

Adam's hatred for me, his deep-seated disgust, was written all over his face as he gazed into my eyes.

"That body right behind you? You know the one, don't you, Stevie? The one that belongs to Win's brother?"

Alarm bells rang in my head, and my pulse roared in my ears and my mouth went dry. "What about him?"

Again, another dumb question. I have no defense for it other than it's some kind of subconscious stall tactic on my part that I can't seem to control.

Adam moved closer to me. His host body, though small, was well muscled, and he cracked his knuckles, staring at me for an intense moment. "It's going to be mine, of course."

And then he snapped his fingers—and everything, the movement outside the window of the room, the flutter of the curtains from the heating register... everything but the machines froze.

Okay, so that was a negatory on dulled magic.

Ten-four, good buddy.

CHAPTER 13

"*M*alutka, look out!*" were the words I heard screaming in my ears directly after Adam shot off a freezing spell and declared Balthazar's body his own.

At first I didn't understand the command from Arkady—until I caught Adam's right hook just under the left side of my chin. He knocked me so hard, with such incredible force, I flew backward and landed on my butt with a crack of bone, crashing into the small chair to the right of the windows.

"No, *malutka*, no! Do not let him get to Zero! Protect Win's body!" Arkady bellowed, just as I was trying to scramble from the floor.

Now, if you're wondering what's going on here, let me just give you a brief overview. Balthazar wasn't officially dead yet, and we still had no idea whether he coded, but I'd bet my eyeteeth Adam was going to make sure he died by pulling the plug on him and jumping into his body at the precise moment of death, before Win could.

Which meant, Win wasn't here yet, and I had no idea where he was.

Which meant I was on my own if I wanted to save this body for Win.

Which I think is the thing I'm supposed to be doing, but I'm not sure.

What I *did* know I was spot-on about was this—if Win tried to get into the body with Adam's healthy, albeit twisted soul already in there, Win's soul was doomed.

So I did what Arkady said and bolted upward from the floor so fast and with such precision, I found myself wishing Win had seen me in action. But my precision didn't last for long, because I was also dead tired and, as a result, dizzy.

The sterile room swam before me, forcing me to steady myself by stretching my hands forward. Still, I only wobbled for a second before I used my thighs and launched myself at Adam's orthopedic-clad feet, sliding across the slick floor on my stomach and gripping his ankle just before he could get his hands on one of the many plugs attached to Win.

With a sharp groan, I gave his ankle the yank of a lifetime, forcing him to fall backward and crash to the ground.

"Good job, *malutka*! Bravo! Now get up and clobber him! You must keep him from Zero at all costs! Get up and give him one in the kisser!"

I did as I was told, the same way I always do, my eyes frantically searching the room for something to use to knock Adam out.

As he skittered across the floor toward the underside of the elderly man's bed, I heard his harsh breathing match my own.

Somewhere in this melee, Belfry appeared and began to pluck at Adam's host body, screeching and swatting at his head and face with his wings. Blood dripped down Adam's face into his eyes, making him howl in anger as I grabbed the first thing I could find to whack him over the head while he was still vulnerable on the ground.

Okay, it happened to be a bedpan, but beggars and choosers, right? It was heavy and hard and that was all I needed.

As Bel attacked and Arkady instructed him about weak points on the body, the cords from the elderly gentleman's monitors catching on the soles of Adam's shoes, I lifted my hands high, the bedpan poised and ready to take his head off, when all manner of lights and screeching warning sounds went off.

I'm not sure where my head was at, but I was so startled, I fumbled that stupid bedpan like a football player fumbles the ball. It fell to the ground and rattled, rocking back and forth in a loud clatter.

That gave Adam the opportunity he needed to rise to his feet, using one of his hands to swipe at Belfry, successfully grabbing him and holding him up high in the air as though he were the prize sacrifice in some ritual.

"Get off me, you mongrel!" he howled, his borrowed face red and lathered with sweat.

"Belfry!" I screamed in fear, as he lobbed my little familiar across the room at the wall with a velocity so forceful, I heard the whistle of the wind it created.

I heard Bel squeal, heard the *thud* of his small body against the wall, watched in horror as he slid down that wall and fell to the ground...

And I became enraged.

As Adam moved closer to Win's bed, he snapped his fingers once more, quieting the machines going off and the ruckus of sound coming from the machinery, his gaze dead as he stared at me.

My eyes flew to the man in the bed across from Win as I huffed and puffed, and I realized in our scuffle, we must have knocked a plug from the wall. Without the aid of the machines, the frail man would die.

"*Malutka*, you must be ready! Pay attention, sweet one. Do not allow him near Zero!"

But Adam laughed as he inched closer, knowing a man was dying right next to him. I know I shouldn't have been surprised. This was a man who'd allowed his child to suffer in order to save his hide. But as the man began to turn blue, his weak body thrashing on the bed, I knew I had to do something. I couldn't just watch this man die.

But Adam backed up and bent at the waist, picking

up one of the plugs and waving it at me like a flag. "What are you gonna do now, do-gooder?" he sneered at me, his voice full of venom.

My chest expanded and threatened to explode, and as I was about to attempt one of my infamous steamrolls to his gut, I heard Arkady scream, "No, Zero! *Nooo!* That is wrong body!"

I blinked, caught completely off guard by Arkady's words and unsure what was happening.

"*Malutka*! Stop Win! You cannot see him, but you must stop him! He is getting into old man's body!"

Holy crab cakes, no!

It was in that split second that I made a decision, one I might have battled longer over if not for the immediacy of the situation.

"My lamb, you must steamroll now! Knock the plug from his hand. Save the old man!" And then he yelled another command, "Zero, *stop!*"

I'm not exactly sure what or how long it takes to get into a body you plan to possess, but I'd sure like to see it one day, because as Arkady was screaming at Win and I was gearing up for a good old-fashioned head plow, he was *still* getting into the wrong body.

"Go, Stevie, go!"

On command, I bent at the waist, inhaled and rushed forward, using my head as a battering ram.

"Belfry!" Arkady bellowed like thunder. "Belfry, get the plug! Plug him back in!" I heard Arkady howl in anguish. "Zero, no! Wait!"

As I rushed Adam, hitting him square in the gut,

every kind of chaos happened all at once—me plowing into Adam and somehow knocking that infernal plug from his hand, and Belfry, clearly revived, swooping over to plug the elderly man back in.

Adam and I fell to the floor seconds after he dropped the plug, and I was on him like fried on chicken, my arms on fire, my legs riddled with cramps so intense, my toes were curling. But I had to keep him from getting to Win, and I had to get Win out of this poor man's body before he ruined it forever.

Sweat dripped between my shoulder blades, my entire body aching from the struggle, but I somehow maneuvered him to his back with a triumphant roar.

Straddling his waist with my legs, I clamped my fists together and wound up, with the intention of bringing them down hard on his forehead, but Adam was too quick for me. He reached upward and grabbed my wrists, rolling me to my back, leaving me almost helpless.

"I'll kill you!" he shrieked, his face a mask of unmistakable rage, his mouth open wide, his spit spraying my face.

"*Malutka*, use your feet! Rear up with hips like Win teach you!"

Planting my feet firmly on the ground, I used all my strength to push upward until I screamed out from the burn in my muscles, but Adam had me, and he wasn't letting go.

"*What do you want from me?*" I yowled from a clenched jaw as the rush of my heart pounding roared in my ears. "Why won't you leave me alone? Why are you torturing me this way?"

Adam never faltered. He never even flinched when he seethed, "Because I can, Stevie! Because I can and I'll never stop until you're dead!"

Then he cackled at my attempts to free myself as thick red lashes from the twist of my skin formed on my wrists from his steel-like grasp.

I fought beneath him, twisting and turning, my breathing harsh and choppy, but I still managed to scream, "Let go, Adam! Let me go!"

That was when he yanked me toward him so hard, I lost the grip my heels had on the floor.

His eyes glittered, hard like bits of black coal, his chest rose and fell, his nostrils flared. "You interfering little fool! Do you really think you can stop me?" he seethed down at me, before he tossed me backward with the strength of someone far larger. "I'll never leave you alone. *Never!*"

I'm telling you, if there were ever a useless sack of potatoes, I was it. I floundered to the floor, flopping around dizzy and disoriented, the wind knocked right out of me, crashing into whatever was in my path.

"Stevie! Stevie, get up! He will pull plug! *You must get up!*"

Panic set in, panic and sheer adrenaline. Somehow, I clawed my way off that floor, my heart beating hard enough to push its way out of my chest, my every muscle like melted butter, but I rose on legs ready to give out.

Adam had squirmed away from me, pulling himself on his stomach toward Balthazar's bed, inching ever closer to disconnect the cord to the life-support machine. When his wide hand was but inches from the plug, I saw red.

This man—this warlock—was a monster. He'd been allowed to go unchecked in and out of the afterlife for far too long, and I wanted him *gone*. I wanted him to hurt like I hurt. I wanted him to die a thousand deaths in agonizing, writhing pain.

But for the moment, I'd settle for getting him away from that plug.

From somewhere deep inside, somewhere primal and red-hot with hatred, I imploded from the inside out.

With a screech of my long pent-up rage, I threw myself at his back, landing with a breath-stealing *thunk* and, reaching for his arm, I drove my fingernails into it, digging into his hard flesh.

His scream of pain brought me deep satisfaction, but I wanted more. I wanted him to suffer—suffer and suffer over and over.

Opening my mouth wide, I jammed my teeth into his shoulder and bit down to the tune of more satisfying wailing.

Just as I wallowed in the sound of his agony, another alarm went off again—and Adam went limp beneath me.

Or should I say, his host body went limp, and you know what that means, right?

His soul was out of one body…and ready to find a new host.

"*Malutka*, no, no, no! Balthazar is dying!"

Using my palms to shove off Adam's host body, I stumbled to stand, catching a glimpse of Balthazar's heart monitor flat-lining, and felt my stomach drop.

This was also my first glimpse of Win, or Balthazar, or whoever, connected to tubes and monitors, helplessly immobile. My heart constricted—and I realized Arkady was right.

I shouldn't have looked at Win.

"Stevie! You must stop this—stop this now!"

"Where is Win? Win! Where are you?" I screamed up into the room, tasting blood on my lip.

"Win! Nooo, Zero! You must wait!" Arkady cried out. "Wait for my signal! No, Win, no!

"Arkady, where's Win?" I screamed, my eyes frantically searching for a soul I couldn't see. But that wasn't the worst of it.

For as long as I live, I'll never forget how Arkady's next words chilled me to the bone.

"Stevie! You must stop him! Adam is stealing Win's body!"

"*How? I don't know how!*" I sobbed over the blare of the machine's alarms, my head spinning. I didn't know what to do. *What should I do?*

Honestly, at that point, I could have collapsed. Not just from exhaustion, but from the sheer force of nature determined to see my butt whooped before it took everything away from me again. How the frickin' frack was I supposed to fight a foe I couldn't see?

"You must stop Adam, Stevie!" Arkady hollered, his voice rolling around the room in an echo so loud, my ears hurt.

Gripping the edge of the bed, I screamed in frustration, "I can't see him, Arkady! What do I do?"

"He is climbing into Balthazar's body, Stevie! Bad man almost in body! We have to do something! Get him out of body! Think, Stevie, think!"

But how? What the heck could I do? My panic swelled like a tide, rushing up to my throat and threatening to choke me. I didn't know how to stop something I couldn't see.

"Zero, no! You cannot!"

That, of all unfortunate times, was it finally hit me. Win was here. *Here*. As in, we were on the same earthly plane. *Together*. Finally—and by hell, I wasn't going to let anyone take that from me.

A warmth washed over me in that defining moment, followed by a swift shot of adrenaline. Suddenly, knowing Win was in the same room, knowing his spirit was here, gave me strength I didn't know I had left.

As the monitors screeched, as the blood drained from my face, as my legs wobbled and I could hardly breathe, I did the only thing I could think of.

I visualized what it would be like for someone to climb into someone else's body and I gave that hospital bed the shove of a lifetime, jerking it forward before pulling it back toward me with a white-knuckled grip.

Tubes flew, machinery crashed, Belfry flew about the room yelling at Win right along with Arkady.

"Winterbutt! Winterbutt! Winterbutt!" Bel screeched and flapped his wings

"Zero, you must get in now! Push him out of way and do it *nooow!*" I heard Arkady cry out, but I was focused on Win—on really seeing Win for the first time.

"Get out!" I screamed at Adam as tears flowed down my face and I climbed onto the bed, dragging Balthazar's body to my chest, pulling him to me, angling his body away from where I visualized Adam would place his. "*Get out!*"

I clung to this big, strong, totally foreign body, wrapping my arms around his broad shoulders and rocking him to and fro. Sweat dripped from my forehead, my eyes stung from more salty tears, my arms ached, but I didn't let go. I wouldn't let go.

Everything stilled then—before there was a loud, horrifying shriek. A blood-curdling howl of rage that scored me to the core with the withering, dying sound of a demonized soul leaving this Earth.

At least for now, anyway.

Whatever magic Adam had used to still the machines must have evaporated, along with the mess we'd made as we'd brawled, because when I opened my eyes, everything was in its rightful place. Even the doctor's body shimmered for a moment before disappearing entirely.

I don't know how, and I won't ask why, but I was grateful I didn't have to clean up the mess or explain why I was in a hospital room with a dead doctor on the floor while I rocked a man I didn't even know in my arms, dressed in scrubs surely spattered with the blood of my enemy.

"Win?" I sobbed hoarsely against the top of his head, my throat raw as he lay limp in my embrace. But I rocked him for all I was worth, closing my eyes again and urging him to answer. "Win, are you in there? Oh, goddess, tell me you're in there!"

A hand...a broad, cool hand...reached up behind me and rested for the briefest moment on my waist before it fell to the bed with a *thump*.

"My dove," a voice whispered, a husky, whiskey-dipped voice with a British accent. "About Thanksgiving dinner..."

CHAPTER 14

"Win? Oh, my goddess, is it really you?" I squeaked the words, still not believing they were real—that *he* was real.

"'Tis indeed, Stephania," he whispered groggily, entwining his fingers with mine. His grip was weak, but it was there. He was there—*here*—in a hospital bed in Chicago, Illinois.

Alive.

And he looked exactly like the picture I had of him and Miranda in Paris—perfect in every way, his classically handsome yet at the same time rugged features more vivid than I could have ever imagined in my head.

I knew this was Balthazar's body, but it had a different vibe to it with Win's spirit embedded in his brother's flesh. Yes, Balthazar looked exactly like Win, but this was no longer the cruel, angry man I'd met who'd wanted to take all of his brother's money and claim it for his own.

Bel flew directly at him, landing on his forehead and pecking his face with affection. "It's you! It's you! It's really you!" he said on a laugh, making loud kissing noises.

Win chuckled, lifting a hand to run his index finger down Bel's tiny head. "Indeed, good man. 'Tis I. How fare thee, my friend?"

Bel giggled and rolled down Win's face. "Thee fares better than he has in a long time, chap. Welcome to my neck of the woods, pal!"

"Thank you, chap," Win whispered, his eyes smiling. "Thank you for all you've done. And you, too, Arkady."

Bel flapped a dismissive wing. "It was nothin', right, Arkady?"

"My friend," Arkady said, deep and low, a hitch in his voice. "Arkady is so happy for you and my *malutka*. I will miss our chats by waterfall, but I am so happy. So, so happy."

"Bah! Are you crying, old man?"

"I no cry. You cry," he teased with a deep chuckle.

And Win laughed with him. "I'll always have time to chat with you, dear friend."

"Okey-doke, wing-ed one. Let us leave our friends to be alone and we go look at pretty nurses, *dah?*"

"*Dah!*" Bel agreed, flying up near the ceiling and swooping down to the floor to skitter under the door.

Climbing off the bed, I repositioned it and grabbed

the chair from the corner of the room. I reached a trembling hand out to stroke his thick, dark hair, shaggy from lack of a trim. I couldn't believe how beautiful he was to look at; how, even after being in a hospital bed in a coma while his life hung in the balance, his brother's body looked healthy and strong.

Yet, even as I marveled at how good he looked, I was still hesitant. I'd been tricked before. How could I know for sure this was really *my* Win? The man I'd spent two and a half years of my life with but had never laid eyes on for more than a few seconds? The man who spoiled me rotten while keeping me on the straight and narrow? The man I'd shared nearly all aspects of my life with?

The man I loved so deeply, but had never believed there was a shred of hope we'd ever share the same space.

How could I know this was really him, and not some cruel spirit playing tricks on us?

Win pulled me to him, his grip ironically firm after such a horrible accident. "*Dove.*" He husked the word against the top of my head. "I call you my dove, and you eat food only a Philistine would eat."

I might have laughed out loud at how easily he read my doubts. Instead, I inhaled sharply, my eyes roaming over his handsome face, over the dark stubble on his chin, searching his half-opened sapphire-blue eyes.

"What...what kind of food?" I asked, my throat so tight it felt as though it might burst.

"Cheese in a can and cake wrapped in..." He stopped and coughed, pressing his free hand to his broad chest. "Wrapped in foil. It's hedonistic."

"But everyone knows that about me," I said, my words thick, almost choking me.

I knew I was testing him, but I was too afraid to trust. I was petrified to trust this was really Win.

"But does everyone call you a Philistine because of your twelve-year-old taste buds, my dove? Do they blindly suffer your love of *My Big Fat Gypsy Wedding* and *90 Day Fiancé*? Do they know you have a friend possessed by a demon, who in turn has a demon friend named Coop? Do they know you accused Sardine of being unable to pronounce radicchio?"

No one called Sandwich Sardine but Win. *No one.*

I blinked back a flood of tears as my heart crashed against my ribs and every muscle in my body shuddered. "*You're here,*" I whispered in awe, my fingers trembling. "You really did it. I can't believe you did it."

With his eyes closed, he smiled weakly. "*You* did it, Dove. You saved me when I couldn't save myself. You truly are a mini-spy. That was quite a display of just how fiercely strong you've become. You and Arkady and Bel were bloody *brilliant*."

I had so many questions, so many things I wanted to say, but I refrained. Surely he needed to rest.

Leaning into him, I cupped his stubbled chin with my hand, using my thumb to stroke his rough skin. "No more talking. You need to rest. You just possessed a body, for gravy's sake. That can't be a walk in the park. We can talk about this once you're better."

He opened his eyes and gazed at me, soft and warm. "No. I need to hear your voice right now. It reminds me my mission is accomplished. Besides, you're practically a walking question mark."

"But I really can wait," I teased, poking his arm (Win's arm!). "I wouldn't want to hinder your progress. This body...er, your new body's been in a coma for a while. It's probably weak. And anyway, I've grown used to waiting for you, Spy Guy. What's a few days more?"

When I've waited a lifetime...

He smirked, making grooves on either side of his mouth stand out. "Now you're just being obtuse. You truly can't wait, Stephania. Who knows that better than I? You have a thousand and one questions for me. Ask away. If I nod off, we can finish this later. Deal?"

I clenched my fist to contain my excitement. I did have a thousand and one questions, maybe even a thousand and two. "Okay, but if you look taxed in any way, game over, pal."

"You, my mini-spy, have yourself a deal."

I grinned down at him. "How, Win? *How* did you do this? Do you have any idea how afraid I was you were gone for good? Why didn't you tell me about Balthazar's coma?"

"What would you have said, Dove? Would you have told me how dangerous the mission would be? Would you have warned me of all the pitfalls? Would you have discouraged me from taking such a risk?"

I poked him in the chest, suddenly angry for what could have happened. "*Yes*! Do you have any idea how south this could have gone? You *did* just see Adam fight you for this body, didn't you? If possession isn't done at exactly the right time, you could have lost your soul."

He managed to lift a hand and press his knuckles to my cheek. "But I didn't, Stephania...and now I can see your beautiful face in person."

My cheeks stung, and I know they turned bright red. I was anything but beautiful after a few sleepless days and a battle royal with a vengeful warlock.

"How did you know Balthazar was in a coma? How did you know he was dying in the first place?"

Stirring, he shifted a bit on the bed in an attempt to sit up, but I placed a flat palm to his muscled chest, urging him to stay put. "There's something to be said for all the hullabaloo about twins, Dove. How they're intertwined in a spiritual way. I'd never in my life felt it until I saw him that first time, when he came and attempted to steal everything from you. Since then, we've been...*connected*. That's the only way I can describe it." His handsome face grew pained when he spoke the words, the deep grooves on either side of his mouth deepening, making me begin another protest.

I was terrified he'd slip away again if we didn't do everything in our power to keep this body safe. "Okay. No more. All this can wait until later. You need to rest, Win."

"*No*," he said, this time a little stronger than the last. "I fear I may do quite a bit of resting as I adjust to this…to my *brother's* body, but truly, I feel quite well for someone who has a fractured skull and was in a coma on, I'm assuming, life support. Is that what all the tubes are about?" He held up one half lying on his chest.

"Yes, and when the night nurses come to check on you, we're in deep dung, buddy. How can we explain yanking a tube from your throat?"

"I'm a spy…an ex-spy, that is. I'll figure it out. Now, I know you have more questions about where I've been since we were arguing over the menu for Thanksgiving. I saw you, Stephania. I watched as you looked for me, as you suffered. I can't bear that you suffered."

My heart skipped several beats when I remembered how dreadful that feeling had been, but I swallowed the memory of that agonizing fear.

Closing my eyes, I swallowed back the hollow emotion and focused on Win's request. "Where did you go after you disappeared?"

With the soft light above the bed showcasing his face, Win appeared almost driven to talk about his experience. "When I found out Balthazar's life hung in the balance, I plane hopped—"

My gasp was sharp, but he squeezed my hand with his warm one to reassure me. "I know how dangerous that sounds, but is it any more dangerous than chasing a Libyan spy whilst hanging from a helicopter over the Indian Ocean? I think not."

I was almost breathless, yet somehow I managed to find a retort. "Chasing a Libyan spy isn't quite the same as risking your soul, Crispin Alistair Winterbottom."

He grinned, and heaven save me, it was devastatingly handsome. "Ah, but alas, here I am, yes? Now, pipe down, mini-spy and let me explain."

I made a face at him and rolled my eyes and suddenly, it was just like old times. "Do carry on, Mr. Fancy Pants."

"Where was I?"

"Risking your soul by plane hopping, you nutter."

He chuckled, deep and husky. "Yes. I plane hopped against your wishes, but I had a gut feeling, Stephania. Much like you, it's something I never ignore. Regardless, knowing Balthazar was on death's door made the risk worth taking. It was my one shot to come back here with little to no repercussions. My twin had no family to speak of, no ties to anyone."

"The body-hopping code?" I asked.

Win swallowed, his Adam's apple working the length of his strong neck. "Yes. I had a strict code, and I stuck to that code. Anyway, I knew he was in distress due to our connection. I knew Balthazar was essentially brain dead, and that meant the doctors would decide to take him off life support. I also knew it wouldn't be long. So I made the leap, and while I waited out Balthazar's fate, I hid from plane to plane, watching and waiting."

"So you really could see us?"

Now he reached out a hand and cupped my chin, running his thumb over my lower lip. "I could. I could see *you*, Dove. All I could see was you."

Which meant he saw me melt down. He saw me begging Baba to help me find him.

I fought to speak, to explain that terrible, horrible moment when I was convinced I'd never see him again, but he pressed a finger against my lips.

"No, Stephania. No explanation required. Had it been you, I can't promise I wouldn't have reacted the same way—done the very same things."

I snorted a watery snort of sarcasm. "Right. International Man of Mystery has snotty, tear-filled breakdown. News at eleven. Not."

His grip on my chin grew firmer, and his next words were fierce. "Please don't dismiss this—don't dismiss what you did. You were afraid. I was unable to ease your fears. It was dreadful, not only to be the cause of your terror, but to be incapable of soothing you. I didn't know how much longer I could wait for Balthazar's soul to be free from his body before I bloody cracked."

His husky words had so many emotions racing through me, leaving me hot and cold and exhilarated and a little frightened, that I had to redirect—to deflect because the intensity threatened to knock the wind out of me.

"So you were the one who sent me the messages? Because listen here, buddy, if you were in charge of communications at MI6, I bet you didn't get any promotions. I mean, *look for bath?*"

His look of concern turned to laughter. "Still as

funny as ever, Stephania." Then he cleared his throat. "No. I wasn't doing the actual physical communicating. Other souls were doing it in my stead at my direction. Hence the sheer chaos and confusion."

"Other souls?"

"Some too nefarious to mention," he said dryly, making it sound as though that were a conversation for another day.

I gasped, my tired, burning eyes going wide. "You were on Plane Eleven, weren't you? Oh, Win, I could kill you!"

"Well, that's already been done, hasn't it?"

I narrowed my eyes at him. "You save the jokey-jokes, mister. If you weren't in such rough shape, I'd clock you one. Do you have any idea how dangerous Plane Eleven is?"

"But look where it brought me, Stephania. It brought me here—to *you*. If the messages were a little rough—"

"A little rough? I repeat, *look for bath?*" I squealed in outrage.

"Is it my fault Louie Lamont from the infamous Lamont mob family can't spell? He forgot the L in Balt-hazar and lost sight of our goal halfway through the task of writing the bloody message. He's utterly impossible to contain."

I stopped cold and gave him a blank stare. "Wait. You mean Louie Lamont...the mobster-from-the-nine-teen-twenties Louie Lamont? Seriously?"

"*Seriously*," he drawled. "Anyway, they were disjointed because they had to be done on the sly, so as not to send out a disturbance in the force. But the cast of characters, whom I shall forever be indebted to, weren't exactly ideal. I didn't handpick them, Stephania. I simply latched on to whomever would listen and help me get to you."

But all I heard were the words "disturbance in the force." Now *this* I understood from my days as a witch. "This disturbance... You mean the keepers of the realms, don't you? The parties responsible for keeping errant souls in line while they choose whether or not to cross?"

"Yes, those. Quite the lot, those errant souls. Most of them terrified to leave the plane due to their earthly misdeeds, for fear what awaits them is less than exemplary on the other side."

I had to close my eyes and take deep breaths. If he had any idea how dangerous this crazy idea had been...

"There, there," he soothed. "Don't fret. I know how dangerous it was, Dove. I know I risked memory loss, among other trying issues. It's why I didn't tell you my plan. Neither here nor there, now."

"So I'm guessing you couldn't put these spirits in touch with Arkady, so he could pass things on to me the way you do when we do a reading?"

"Correct. They're chained to their appointed planes until they decide."

"Unlike you, Plane Hopper," I teased, adjusting to the enormity of what he'd done.

He closed his eyes again and hunkered down under the sterile blankets with a smug grin. "Unlike me, their risks aren't worth the rewards. Mine was."

Sitting up, I brushed my hands together and tucked the blanket under his chin. "Okay, enough for now. You need to rest this new body of yours. It won't work the way yours did, and I feel a big adjustment coming on." Boy, if he only knew how weird this was going to be.

"But don't you want to know about the clues I sent you? Come, Stephania. You know you do, and I promise you. I'm fine. Wonderful, in fact."

Of course I did, but I wanted him well more.

He ran a finger down the tip of my nose. "Stephania? Please, carry on."

At his urging, I decided to go along with him until I saw signs of real strain or we were busted by the nurses. "Okay, I managed to figure out a couple of them, like the postcard. But the pizza? Whew boy, that one really had me going. You had someone order me a deep-dish pizza because Balthazar was in Chicago, right?"

"Wrong," he said flatly. "You needed to nourish yourself, Stephania. You hadn't eaten all day, for pity's sake, and I know pizza is one of your favorites. Gerta was happy to help me see you fed."

I frowned. "Gerta?"

"The spirit who called in the order to Petey's and pretended to be you, of course. It wasn't originally going to be a clue. That was the lovely Gerta's idea, and you have to admit, sending you a deep-dish pizza to represent Chicago was rather clever."

"So spirits have cell phones these days?"

"Not exactly," he said on a husky chuckle, the one that always made me smile. "Though, it would seem they can borrow one here on Earth."

I was so disappointed in myself for not catching on sooner, I could scream. "I can't believe I missed that. It went right over my head. But then, I missed plenty. Except for the Vivaldi reference. That one was easy. Oh, and by the way, your friend with the postcard? He almost owed me an Hermes scarf—vintage. It was this close to totally ruined."

Win winced and gave me a sheepish grin. "Ah, yes. Moe. I'm sorry he was so passionate, not to mention dramatic. I mean, really, 'save him'? That was going just a little too far, in my opinion. I didn't need saving...or I didn't think I did. I needed you to know what I was up to."

"*Passionate*? Is that what we're calling what he did to the store? All that just to show me a postcard? Well, let me tell you, Passionate Moe tore the place up, but to his credit, he did put everything back where it belonged."

Win closed his eyes and grinned. "As I soon found, he can be very high-strung when he's making a point. Every contact I made was a roll of the dice, Dove. Every bloody one."

"What about the mustache? Who drew the mustache on fake Win's picture?"

His inhale was deep and sharp. "That was Adam, taunting you, my dove. I'll give you this, he's a worthy foe. I don't know how he found out about Balthazar or how he's able to perform the feats of magic he's capable of, but as I watched you battle him, I'd never felt so helpless in all my life."

"It's over now," I whispered, running my palm over his chest. I didn't want talk of Adam to taint our reunion. "I don't know if it'll always be over, but it is for now. I'm more interested in this rumor about you crossing over. What was that about?"

Now his lips went thin. "Largely just that. A rumor. I did go into a light of sorts, one that leaves a vaporous trail when I jumped from Plane Limbo, this much is true, but as you well know, the spirits are easily confused."

That explained our broken tether. He'd broken it by jumping to another plane.

"I really thought you'd crossed. It was the only logical explanation," I whispered.

"How could you think I'd ever leave you without saying goodbye, Stephania?" Brushing his lips over my knuckles, he whispered, "That will *never* happen."

My cheeks went red and hot again, and my stomach did a backflip off the balance beam. But now it was time to get down to the nitty gritty—the meat of this whole incredible, insane journey.

"And Balthazar? His soul?" I asked softly. I didn't begrudge Win his brother's body if his time here on

Earth was truly up, believe me. I only wish they could have made amends before this happened.

Win paused a moment, his muscular chest expanding as he inhaled. "Damaged beyond repair, Dove. Yet, as we passed one another in the ethereal corridors, moments before I wedged my way into his body, I sensed in him a peace he's never known. And if consent can be given when one takes possession of someone else's being, I believe he gave me his."

A tear threatened to escape my eye. I didn't think I had any left, I'd cried so many, but as a child, Balthazar hadn't been given a shot the way Win had. I mourned for what could have been, and I know Win did, too.

Still, I shook it off with the intent to move forward. "All right, Body Surfer, enough's enough. You need rest. Not to mention, I'm going to be banned from this hospital until kingdom come when the nurses come in here and see you've somehow yanked all your tubes out with a strange woman by your bed. I'm not sure busted is a strong enough word for what we'll be."

His chuckle tickled my ears. "What day is it anyway, Dove? I seem to have lost track."

Looking out the window, the lights from the parking lot below showcasing the snow, I caught my breath when I remembered. It was the most appropriate of day of all. "It's almost Thanksgiving, Win."

"Hmmm," he murmured, letting his eyes slide closed. "And I am deeply thankful."

"Me, too," I whispered, my voice shaky. *Me, too.*

"But I'll admit to some disappointment at missing that lovely feast we planned," he groused.

I smiled in sympathy, patting his chest. "I'm sorry we're going to miss the big feast *you* planned. But I promise, this Christmas will be the best one ever. You can have as much snobby food as you like. Squicky liver paste and all. You won't hear me complain once." Never, ever again.

But Win mocked an exaggerated sigh. "You must be so sad to have missed out on your Cheez Whiz and cardboard crackers, eh? It was the last thing I heard you twittering about before I had to make the leap. I'm sorry it was so sudden, Stephania."

"Don't be sorry. Now, open your eyes and look at me, please." When he did, I grinned down at him in impish delight, pressing his hand to my cheek. "You do know where we are, don't you?"

He gave me an almost startled look. "In a hospital in Chicago. How quickly we forget the deep-dish pizza."

"Uh-huh. We're in Chicago. Home of the Cubs and, indeed, deep-dish pizza, but do you know what Chicago is also home to?"

Now he gave me a hesitant look, his response dry. "Do tell."

I gave him another flirty smile. "The factory where they make Cheez Whiz, of course. Guess what we're having for Thanksgiving dinner, Spy Guy!"

He groaned long and loud before he burst out laughing, the deep vibration of his chuckle filling my ears.

I began to rise, hoping to sneak out before we got caught, but there was one more thing I had to do. Cradling his face, I pressed my nose to his. "Okay, Spy Guy, I have to skedaddle before we start World War III. I need a shower, a change of clothes and a way to pay for it all, because Baba didn't send me with my purse, that dastardly woman. But before I go, I have to tell you something."

Win latched onto my wrists, his warm blue eyes scanning mine. "What's that, Dove?"

I took a deep, shaky breath. I had a promise to myself to keep, and I was going to keep it with no expectations from the reciprocating party.

I'd waited a long time to share my heart, and I'd almost lost the chance entirely. I don't ever want to feel so hollow and alone again.

"I love you, Crispin Alistair Winterbottom—even in someone else's body," I whispered, my eyes welling with hot tears. "I don't know what that means, now that you're no longer an afterlife away. I don't know what will happen from here, but I wanted you to know how I feel so you'll never have to wonder. No matter how many planes you hop."

He narrowed his eyes playfully and dropped a kiss on the tip of my nose. "You do know, you will never— not even with me as a passenger—drive my Aston Martin. Not even if you tell me you love me as a ploy to get your dainty hands on my beautiful car."

My head popped up as I gazed down at his face—his

handsome, perfect, chiseled face—and giggled. "You suck."

His chuckle was deep and rumbling as his blue-blue eyes gazed into mine. "Will I still suck if I tell you I love you, too?"

I grinned at him, dropping a kiss on his cheek. "Maybe not as much. Now about that Aston Martin. Surely we can negotiate?"

"So is Sleeping Beauty still getting his Z's on?" Bel asked as I sat at the kitchen table and watched fat flakes of snow swirl over Puget Sound.

"He is," I answered, taking a sip of my coffee and sighing with happiness at the very unusual but very welcome snow, and right at the beginning of the Christmas season, too.

Win had hardly been awake since we'd brought him home a few days ago, but his body—or Balthazar's body—had been through a trauma, and it would take time to heal. Time that should have been spent in the hospital under the care of trained medical professionals, but Win wouldn't hear of it.

No, he'd had Belfry on the phone and, in a matter of an hour, hired someone to not only transport him back here, but a nurse to care for him while he recuperated.

Same old Win, just here on Earth instead of upstairs in the afterlife.

The doctors had dubbed him a medical miracle, and as we sat and listened to them talk about future therapy and fine motor skills, and give him a good lecture on pulling his tubes out, we secretly smiled over their heads at one another when they told us how lucky we were.

If they only knew...

Apparently, Balthazar had been dropped at the ER by an anonymous source; his skull fractured, his brain swelling, and not expected to live. No one knew what happened to him, but I'd lay bets Win will want to investigate once he's up and about.

As to how we got to the hospital that night, meaning Baba Yaga, I hadn't heard a peep. There'd been no word from that part of my life. So I felt pretty sure I should keep my mouth shut while I counted my blessings and remain silently, eternally thankful.

I could never repay Baba for what she'd done, and I didn't know if I'd have to, but for now, I was going to focus on Win's recovery and figuring out how we were going to deal with this new path our lives had taken.

"Man, he's gonna be on the cover of *GQ* for all the sleep he's getting, huh? Did the doctor say this was normal?"

"Well, I didn't exactly ask him what to expect when you've possessed a body. The doctor says Balthazar was in a coma for almost a week while he remained unidentified. In human terms, it's going to take a little while for him to build up his strength. But I hear through the grapevine, a.k.a. Winnie, it takes a lot of rest to recuperate after a successful possession."

"I keep peeking in to see him when Nurse Ratched isn't looking because I'm afraid he's going to disappear. He's just like I imagined. Tall and fancy and a little rough around the edges, but with a hoity-toity accent." Bel chirped his glowing endorsement. "Can you even believe he's here, Stevie? It's amazing. Just fekkin' incredible."

No. I still couldn't believe it, but every second he slept, every moment we were in the same space together, I spent cherishing his presence. Even from all the way upstairs in the guest bedroom, I felt his strength, his integrity, his determination.

"Nurse Ratched didn't see you, did she? We *do not* need that kind of chaos, buddy."

The nurse Win had hired via Belfry was like the Gestapo. Her name was Gloria, and she kept me from that room the way a cage fighter keeps his opponent at bay because according to her, I was a distraction to Win's recovery. Which, by the by, made me secretly blush almost as much as I'd groused.

"Nope. I was like ninja bat. Swear it."

I chuckled, scooping him up in the palm of my hand and dropping a kiss on his little yellow snout before tucking him against my shoulder. "You're the best thing that's ever happened to me, Belfry. I never could have made it through this without you. And you either, my favorite Russian," I whispered, looking up at the ceiling.

"Ah, *malutka*. I am so happy for you and my Zero. We still make good team, *dah*?"

My heart tightened in my chest in gratitude. "I never could have taken on Adam without you, Arkady, and I never want to. We're always going to be a team for as long as I have any say in the matter."

Nurse Ratched…er, Gloria, poked her head into the kitchen, her glowering face and stout body filling up the entryway. She tucked her purse under her sturdy arm, smoothing a hand over her taupe skirt. "I'm sorry? Did you say something, Miss Cartwright?"

I waved a hand and gave her a sheepish look, covering Bel with the palm of my hand. "Oh, nothing. Just mumbling to myself." Gosh, this woman was a better spy than Win and Arkady put together. I can't tell you how many times she's snuck up on me in a mere two days.

She gave me a curt nod, her lips thinning. "Good enough. I'm off to take my lunch break, Miss Cartwright. I'll see you in exactly one hour." And she meant it, too. If she said an hour, it wouldn't be a second longer.

As Gloria left to take her afternoon break, and I heard her cute compact car zipping out of the driveway, a sudden crash and a weird screech from upstairs had me taking the steps three at a time to head toward Win's room.

I whipped around the corner on the opposite end of the hall from my bedroom, where his den of recuperation was located, and skidded to a halt.

193

My mouth fell open as I stuck my head into Win's room, where he sat amidst a mountain of deep blue and rust-colored pillows. The shades were up, the sheer curtains falling gracefully to the floor, allowing him a view of the snow.

Whiskey lay at his feet, and Strike was in the corner of the room by the gold and burgundy settee under the bay of floor-to-ceiling windows.

"Dove?"

I gulped nervously, jamming my index finger between my teeth as I winced. "International Man of Mystery?"

"Should I be overjoyed to see you've regained some of your powers? Is that what this is?" He pointed to the heavy teak mantel above the fireplace.

I folded my hands together behind my back and winced as, from the vicinity of the fireplace, pieces of a plant flew through the air.

"I don't think I've regained my powers. Not totally, anyway."

Or at least, not the powers I'd once had, because I can assure you, my old powers would *not* have produced something like this—and they wouldn't have produced it days after I'd cast the spell.

It had to be some weird, cosmic fluke. I think. I hope...

Oh, dear.

I didn't know what this meant.

"Ahh, pity that," he said over a loud screech coming from the direction of the fireplace, wearing an amused smile. "Then care to explain what's on the mantel of the fireplace I so lovingly chose brick by brick, and how you propose we shall tell the lovely Nurse Gloria?"

"There's nothing lovely about her," I drawled and wrinkled my nose.

He waggled a lean finger at me in admonishment, his handsome face full of reproach. "Now, now, Stephania," he chided in the way I'd missed so much. "She gets the job done. Isn't that why we hired her? To whip me into shape?"

I made a face at him. "*You* hired her, and she gets the job done if you like forty lashes with your bread and water for dinner."

He chuckled, deep and rumbling, a sound I was growing fonder of each minute he was here. "Never you mind. She's the woman who's going to have me on my feet in no time flat. I quite like a rigid bout of training."

It had been hard to get Win to come to terms with the idea that he was no longer in the condition he'd once been. Sure, Balthazar's body was in great shape, but it probably wouldn't have the muscle memory and reflexes Win had. In other words, James Bond was going to have to slow his roll when he was finally on his feet.

I clucked my tongue. "First of all, even Nurse *American Horror Story* said it's going to take time for you to build up your strength, ex-spy. Secondly, this isn't *training*. You're not in the body of a spy anymore. You're recuperating. There's a difference."

Sighing, now he rolled his eyes at me. I'm sure he'd had it up to his snooty British eyeballs with us insisting he rest, but that was too bad. He was here, and I wasn't going to risk losing him again. *Ever*.

"That's not what we're here to discuss, Dove." He waved his hands once more in the direction of the mantel. "Now, are you going to explain?" he asked, then winced at the loud howl of sound filling the bedroom.

I waited for the screeching to come down a notch before I asked, "Explain? As in, tell you the details about how *that* ended up in your room?"

"Yes. *That*," he answered dryly, one eyebrow raised. "That being a lesothosaurus, for your information. A compact little bugger of a dinosaur at about three feet tall with bloody sharp teeth—an herbivore, to be precise, and bi-pedal, in that he runs on two feet."

I blinked as I stooped to pick up the pieces of the plant the small dinosaur was spraying about as he gnawed on it with voracious glee. "Wow. You sure know your dinosaurs, huh?"

Win winked at me with one luscious eye. "I was nothing if not a scholarly boy."

"He's actually kind of cute, don't you think?"

"As in Whiskey cute, Stephania? Nay. Nay, he is most certainly not cute, and I don't suggest getting him a heated bed and a bowl with his name on it."

I gave Win my best pouty look. "Dinosaurs need love, too."

The lesothosaurus let out another screechy howl,

but he appeared content to chew on the Christmas cactus on the mantel—for the moment.

"Ah, but do they need the kind of love we can give them, Stephania?"

"Aw, c'mon, Spy Guy. He's not so bad in a lizardy sort of way."

He peered at me with one eye, the other narrowed as he popped his lips. Lifting his square jaw, he said, "Stephania, enough soft shoe. Details, please."

I winced again, tucking my hair behind my ears in a nervous gesture. "Got a minute?"

Win patted the space next to him on the bed with a grin that grew stronger every day. "I have all the time in the world, Dove. Do share with the rest of the class."

I giggled as I slipped into the room and perched on the edge of his lush king-size bed. "So, it went something like this. There's this little thing called a time-travel spell...or maybe it was the conjuring spell... I can't say for sure, but I tried 'em all—gave 'em heck, I did. I can't believe you missed that part of the show while you were plane hopping. Anyway..."

And as I explained, with our fingers intertwined, and the soft pitter-patter of the snow prancing against the windows, Belfry flew past the guest bedroom, whistling the tune to "So This is Love."

And I thought, yes.

Yes. This *is* love.

The End

(Thank you for joining me for yet another edition of *Witchless in Seattle Mysteries*—I so hope you enjoyed the newest journey for Stevie and Win, but hang on to your Cheez Whiz, because it ain't over yet! Come back in 2019 for more crazy adventures, more twists and turns than a roller coaster, but most of all, just come back now, ya hear?)

Chapter 1

"So, Sister Trixie Lavender, how do we feel about this space? Open concept, with plenty of sprawling views of the crumbling sidewalk from the leaky picture window and easily room for eight tat chairs.

"Also, one half bathroom for customers, one full for us—which means we'd have to share, but there are worse things. A bedroom right up those sketchy stairs with a small loft, which BTW, I'm calling as mine now. I like to be up high for the best possible views when I survey our pending tattoo empire. A tiny kitchenette, but no big deal. I don't cook anyway, and *you* sure don't, if that horse pucky you called oatmeal is any indication of your culinary skills. Lots of peeling paint and crappy plumbing. All for the low-low price of...er, what was that price again, Fergus McDuff?"

Short and chubby, a balding Fergus McDuff, the landlord of the current dive I was assessing as a candidate for our tattoo parlor, cringed and visibly shuddered beneath his limp blue suit.

Maybe because Coop had him up against a wall, holding him by the front of his shirt in white-knuckled fists as she waited for him to rethink the price he'd quoted us the moment he realized we were women.

Which was not only an outrageous amount of money for this dank, pile-of-rubble hole in the wall, but not at all the amount quoted to us over the phone. It also looked nothing like the picture from his Facebook page. I know that shouldn't surprise me. He'd probably used some Snapchat filter to brighten it up. But here we were.

A bead of perspiration popped out just above Fergus's thin upper lip.

Coop's dusky auburn hair curtained her face, but his stance remained firm. "Like I said, lady, it's three grand a month—"

Cutting his words off, Coop tightened her grip with a grunt and hauled Fergus higher. His pleading gray eyes darted from her to me and back again in unadulterated fear, but to his credit, he tried really hard not to show it.

Coop licked her lips, a low hum of a growl coming from her throat, her gaze intently focused on poor Fergus. "Can I kill him, Sister Trixie Lavender? Please, please, pleeease?"

"*Coop*," I warned. She knew better than to ask such a question. "She's just joking, Fergus. Promise."

"But I'm not. Though, I promise I'll clean up afterward. It'll be like it never happened—"

"Two thousand!" Fergus shouted quite jarringly, as though the effort to push the words out pained him. "Wait, wait, wait! I meant to say two thousand a month with *all* utilities!"

That's my demon. Overbearing and intimidating as the day is long. Still, I frowned at her, pulling my knit cap down over my ears. While this behavior worked in our favor, it was still unacceptable.

We'd had a run-in with the law a few months ago back in Ebenezer Falls, Washington, where we'd first tried to set up a tattoo shop. Coop's edgy streak had almost landed her with a murder charge.

Since then (and before we landed in Eb Falls, by the by), we'd been traveling through the Pacific Northwest, making ends meet by selling my portrait sketches to people along the way, waiting until Coop's instincts choose the right place for us to call home.

Cobbler Cove struck just the right chord with her. And that's how we ended up here, with her breathing fire down Fergus McDuff's throat.

Coop, who'd caught on to my displeasure, smirked her beautiful smirk and set Fergus down with a gentle drop, brushing his trembling shoulder with a careful hand to smooth his wrinkled suit.

"That's nice. You're being nice, Fergus McDuff. I like you. Do you like me?"

"Coop?" I called from the other end of the room, going over some rough measurements for a countertop in my mind. "Playtime's over, young lady. Let Mr. McDuff be, please."

She rolled her bright green eyes at me in petulance and wiped her hands down her burgundy leather pants, disappointment written all over her face that there'd be no killing today.

Coop huffed. "Fine."

I looked at her with my stern ex-nun's expression as a clear reminder to remember her manners. "Coop…"

She pouted before holding out her hand to Fergus, even though he outwardly cringed at the gesture. "It was nice to meet you, Fergus McDuff. I hope I'll see you again sometime soon," she said almost coquettishly, mostly following the guidelines I'd set forth for polite conversation with new acquaintances.

Fergus brushed her hand away, fear still on his face, and that was when I knew it was time for me to step in.

"You do realize she's just joking—about killing you and all, don't you? I would never let her do that," I joked, hoping he'd come along for the ride.

But he only nodded as Coop picked up his tie clip and handed it to him in a gesture of apology.

I smiled at her and nodded my head in approval, dropping my hands into the pockets of my puffy vest. "Okay, Fergus. Sold. Two grand a month and utilities it is. A year lease, right? Have a contract handy?"

Fergus nodded and scurried toward the front of the store to get his briefcase. It was then Coop leaned toward me and sniffed the air, her delicate nostrils flaring.

"This place smells right, Trixie Lavender. Yes, it does. Also, I like the name Peach Street. That sounds like a nice place to live."

I looked into her beautiful eyes—eyes so green and perfectly almond-shaped they made other women sick with jealousy—and smiled, feeling a sense of relief. "Ya think? You've got a good vibe about it then? Like the one you had in Ebenezer Falls before the bottom fell out?"

And you were accused of murder and our store was left in shambles?

I bit the inside of my cheek to keep from bringing up our last escapade in a suburb of Seattle, with an ex-witch turned medium named Stevie Cartwright and her dead spy turned ghost cohort, Winterbottom. It was still too fresh.

Coop rolled her tongue along the inside of her cheek and scanned the dark, mostly barren space with critical eyes. Any mention of Eb Falls, and Coop grew instantly sullen. "I miss Stevie Cartwright. She said she'd be my friend. Always-always."

My face softened into a smile. I missed Stevie and her ghost compatriot, too. Even though I couldn't actually hear Winterbottom—or Win, as she'd called him—Coop could, and from what she'd relayed to me, he sounded delightfully British and madly in love with Stevie.

Certainly an unrequited love, due to their circumstances—him being all the way up there on what they called Plane Limbo (where souls wait to decide if they wish to cross over)—and Stevie here on Earth, but they fit one another like gloves.

Stevie had been one of the best things to ever happen to me; Coop, too. She'd helped us in more ways than just solving a murder and keeping Coop from going to jail. She'd helped heal our hearts. She'd shown us what it meant to be part of a community. She'd helped us learn to trust not just our instincts, but to let the right people into our lives and openly enjoy their presence.

"Trixie? Do you think Stevie meant we'd always be friends?"

I winked at Coop. "She meant what she said, for sure. She always means what she says. If she said she'll always be your friend, you can count on it. And I miss Stevie, too, Coop. Bet she comes to visit us soon."

Coop almost smirked, which was her version of a smile—something we worked on every day. Facial expressions and body language humans most commonly use.

"Will she eat spaghetti with us?" she asked, referring to the last meal we'd shared with Stevie, when she'd invited her friends over and made us a part of not just her community, but her family.

"I bet she'll eat whatever we make. So anyway… We were talking the vibe here? It feels good to you?"

"Yep. I can tattoo here."

"Gosh, I hope so. We need to plant some roots, Coop. We need to begin again Finnegan."

We needed to find a sense of purpose after Washington, and this felt right. This suburb of Portland called the Cobbler Cove District felt right.

Tucking her waist-length hair behind her ear, Coop nodded her agreement with a vague pop of her lips, the wheels in her mind so obviously turning. "So we can grow and be a part of the community. So we can blend."

"Yes, blending is important. Now, about threatening Fergus…"

Her eyes narrowed on Fergus, who'd taken a phone call and busily paced the length of the front of the store. "He was lying, Trixie Lavender. Three grand wasn't what he said on the phone at all. No, it was not. I know what I heard. You said it's bad to lie. I was only following the rules, just like you told me I should if I wanted to stay here with you and other humans."

Bobbing my head to agree, I pinched her lean cheek with affection and smiled. "That's exactly what I said, Coop. *Exactly*. Good on you for finally listening to me after our millionth conversation about manners."

"Do I win a prize?"

I frowned as I leaned against the peeling yellow wall. I never knew where Coop was going in her head sometimes. She took many encounters, words, people, whatever, at face value. Almost the way a small child would—except this sometime-child had an incredible figure and a savage lust for blood if not carefully monitored.

"A prize, Coop?" I asked curiously, tucking my hands in the pockets of my jeans. "Explain your thinking, please."

She gazed at me in all seriousness as she quite visibly concentrated on her words. I watched her sweet, uncluttered mind put her thoughts together.

"Yep. A prize. I saw it the other day on a sign at the grocery store. The millionth shopper wins free groceries for a year. Do I get something for free after our millionth conversation?"

Laughter bubbled from my throat. Coop didn't just bring me endlessly sticky situations, she brought me endless laughter and, yes, even endless joy. She's simple, and I don't mean she's unintelligent.

I mean, sometimes she's so black and white, I find it hard to explain to her the many levels and nuances of appropriate reactions or emotions for any given situation, and that can tax me on occasion. But she's mine, and she'd saved my life, and I wasn't ever going to forget that.

And I do mean *ever*.

She'd tell you I'd saved *hers*, but that's just her innocent take on a situation that had been almost impossible until she'd shown up with her trusty sword.

I gazed up at the water-stained ceiling and thought about how to explain the complexities of mankind. I decided simple was best.

"Trixie? Do I get a prize?" she inquired again, her tone more insistent this time.

"No free groceries. Just my love and eternal gratitude that you restrained yourself and didn't kill Fergus. He's not a bad man, Coop. And when I say *bad*, I mean the kind of bad who kicks puppies and pulls the wings off moths for sport. He's just trying to make his way in the world and get ahead. Just like everybody else. It might not be nice, but you can't kill him over it. Them's the rules, Demon."

"But he wasn't being fair, Sister Trixie Lavender."

"Remember what we discussed about my name?"

Now she frowned, the lines in her perfectly shaped forehead deepening. "Yes. I forgot—again. You're not a nun anymore and it isn't necessary to call you by your last name. You're just plain Trixie."

Plain Trixie was an understatement. Compared to Coop, Angelina Jolie was plain. My mousy, stick-straight reddish brown (all right, mostly brown) hair and plump thighs were no match for the sleek Coopster. But you couldn't be jealous of her for long because she had no idea how stunning she was, and that was because she didn't care.

"Right. I'm just Trixie. Just like Fergus isn't Fergus McDuff. He's just plain old Fergus, if he allows you to call him by his first name, or Mr. McDuff if he prefers the more formal way to address someone. And I'm not a nun anymore. That's also absolutely right."

My heart shivered with a pang of sadness at that,

but I'm finally able to say that out loud now and actually feel comfortable doing so.

I wasn't a nun anymore, and I'm truly, deeply at peace with the notion. My faith had become a bone of contention for me long before I'd exited the convent, so it was probably better I'd ended up being kicked out on my ear any ol' way.

In fact, I often wonder if it hadn't *always* been a bone of contention for the entire fifteen years I'd lived there. I'd always questioned some of the rules.

I'd never wanted to enter the convent to begin with —my parents put me there when they could no longer handle my teenage substance abuse. They'd left me in the capable, nurturing hands of my mother's dear friend, Sister Alice Catherine.

But after I'd kicked my drug habit, and decided to take my vows in gratitude for all the nuns of Saint Aloysius By The Sea had done for me, I came to love the thick stone walls, the soft hum and tinkle of wind chimes, and the structure of timely prayer.

They'd saved me from my addiction. In their esteemed honor, I wanted to save people, too. What better way to do so than becoming a nun in dedicated service to the man upstairs?

Though, I can promise you, I didn't want to leave the convent the way I did. A graceful exit would have been my preferred avenue of departure.

Instead, I left by way of possession. Yes. I said *possession*. An ugly, fiery, gaping-black-mouthed, demonic possession. I know that's a lot of adjectives, but it best describes what wormed its way inside me on that awful, horrible night.

"Are you sad now, Trixie? Did I make you sad because you aren't a nun anymore?" Coop asked, very clearly worried she'd displeased me—which did happen from time to time.

For instance, when she threatened to kill anyone who even looked cross-eyed at me—sometimes if they just breathed the wrong way.

I had to remind myself often, it was out of the goodness of her heart she'd nearly severed a careless driver's head when he'd encroached on our pedestrian right of way (the pedestrian always has the right of way in Portland, in case you were wondering). Or lopped off a man's fingers with a nearby butter knife for grazing my backside by accident while we were in a questionable bar.

Still, even while Coop's emotions ruled her actions without any tempered, well-thought-out responses, she was a sparkling diamond in the rough, a veritable sponge, waiting to soak up all available knowledge.

I tugged at a lock of her silky hair, shaking off the memory of that night. "How can I be sad if I have you, Coop DeVille?"

She grimaced—my feisty, compulsive, loveable demon grimaced—which is her second version of a smile (again, she's still practicing smiling. There's not much to smile about in Hell, I suppose) and patted my cheek—just like I'd taught her. "Good."

"So, do you think you're up to the task of some remodeling? This place is kind of a mess."

Actually, it was a disaster. Everything was crumbling. From the bathroom that looked as though it hadn't been cleaned since the last century, to the peeling walls and yellowed linoleum with holes all throughout the store.

Her expression went thoughtful as she cracked her knuckles. "That means painting and using a hammer, right?"

I brushed my hands together and adjusted my scarf. "Yep. That's what that means, Coop."

"Then no. I don't want to do that."

I barked a laugh, scaring Fergus, who was busily rifling through his briefcase, looking for the contract I'm now positive changes with the applicant's gender.

"Tough petunias. We're in this together, Demon-San. That means the good, the bad, and the renovation of this place. If you want to start tattooing again, we can't have customers subjected to this chaos, can we? Who'd feel comfortable getting a tattoo in a mess like this?"

I pointed to the pile of old pizza boxes and crushed beer cans in the corner where I hoped we'd be able to build a cashier's counter.

Coop's sigh was loud enough to ensure I'd hear it as she let her shoulders slump. "You're right, Sis...um, *Trixie*. We have to have a sterile environment to make tattoos. The Oregon laws say so. I read them, you know. On the laptop. I read them *all*."

As I said, Coop's a veritable sponge, which almost makes up for her lack of emotional control.

Almost.

I patted her shoulder as it poked out of her off-the-shoulder T-shirt, the shoulder with a tattoo of an angel in all its magnificently winged glory. A tattoo she'd drawn and inked herself while deep in the bowels of Hell.

"I'm proud of you. I'm going to need all the help I can get so we can get our license to open ASAP. We need to start making some money, Coop. We don't have much left of the money Sister Mary Ignatius gave us, and we definitely can't live on our charm alone."

"So I've been useful?"

"You're more than useful, Coop. You're my right-hand man. Er, woman."

She grinned, and it was when she grinned like this, when her gorgeously crafted face lit up, I grew more certain she understood how dear a friend she was to me. "Good."

"Okay, so let's go sign our lives away—"

"No!" she whisper-yelled, gripping my wrist with the strength of ten men, her face twisted in fear. "Don't do that, Trixie Lavender! You know what happens when you do that. Nothing is as it seems when you do that!"

I forced myself not to wince when I pried her fingers from my wrist. Sometimes, Coop didn't know her own demonic strength. "Easy, Coop. I need my skin," I teased.

In an instant, she dropped her hands to her sides and shoved them into the pockets of her pants, her expression contrite. "My apologies. But you know I have triggers. That's what you called them, right? When I get upset and anxious, that's a trigger. Signing your life away is one of them. We have to be careful with our words. You said so yourself."

She was right. I'd poorly worded my intent, forgetting her fears about the devil and Hell's shoddy bargains for your soul.

As the rain pounded the roof, I measured my words and tried to make light of the situation. "It's just a saying we use here, Coop. It means we're giving everything we have to Fergus McDuff on a wing and a prayer at this point. But it doesn't mean I'm giving up my soul to the devil. I promise. My soul's staying put."

At least I thought it was. I could be wrong after my showdown with an evil spirit, but it felt like it was still there. I still had empathy for others. I still knew right from wrong—even if all those morals went directly out the window when the evil spirit took over.

Coop inhaled and exhaled before she squared her perfectly proportioned shoulders. "Okay. Then let's go," she paused, frowning, "sign our lives away to Fergus McDuff." Then she smirked, clearly meaning she understood what I'd said.

Our path to Fergus slowed when Coop paused and put a hand on my arm, setting me behind her. There was a commotion of some kind occurring just outside our door on the sidewalk, between Fergus and another man.

A dark-haired man with olive skin stretched tightly over his jaw and sleeve tattoos on both arms yelled down at Fergus, who, after Coop, had probably had enough of being under fire for today. But holy crow, this guy was angry.

He waved those muscular arms—attached to lean hands with long fingers—around in the air as the rain pelted his sleek head. His T-shirt stretched over his muscles as he gestured over his shoulder, and his voice, even muffled, boomed along our tiny street.

I couldn't make out what they were saying, but it didn't look like a very friendly exchange—not judging by the man's face, which, when it wasn't screwed up in anger, was quite handsome.

Yet, Fergus, clearly at his breaking point after his encounter with Coop, reared up in the gentleman's face and yelled right back. But then a taller, leaner, sandy-haired man approached and put a hand on the handsome man's shoulder, encouraging him to turn around.

That gave Fergus the opportunity to push his way past the big man and grab the handle of our door, stepping back inside the store with a bluster of huffs and grunts.

Coop sniffed the air. She can sometimes smell things the rest of us can't. It's hard to explain, but as an example, she smelled that our friend Stevie isn't entirely human. She's a witch. Or she was. Now, since her accident, she only has some residual powers left.

But Coop had smelled her paranormal nature somehow—which, by definition, is crazy incredible and something I can't dwell on for long, for fear I'll get lost in the madness that demons and Hell and witches and other assorted ghouls are quite real.

"The man outside is not paranormal. He's just normal, as is the other man, and Fergus, too. If you were wondering."

I popped my lips in Coop's direction. "Good to know. I mean, what if he was some crazy hybrid of a vampire who can run around in daylight? Then what? We'd have to keep our veins covered or he might suck us dry."

Coop gave me her most serious expression and sucked in her cheeks. "I already told you, you don't ever have to worry anyone will hurt you. I'll kill them and then they'll be dead."

Ba-dump-bump.

"And I told *you*, no killing." Then I giggled and wrapped an arm around her shoulder, steering her past the debris on the floor and toward a grumpy Fergus, feeling better than I had in weeks. We had a purpose. We had a mission. Above all, we had hope.

We were going to open Inkerbelle's Tattoos and Piercings. I'd pierce and design tattoos, and Coop would handle the rest. We'd hopefully hire a staff of more artists as gifted as Coop. If the universe saw fit, that is.

And then maybe we'd finally have a place to call home. Where I could nest, and Coop could ink to her heart's desire in her tireless effort to protect every single future client from demonic harm with her special brand of magic ink.

During her life under Satan's rule, Coop had tattooed all new entries into Hell. She'd been so good at it, the devil left her in charge of every incoming sinner. But it was a job she'd despised, and she eventually escaped the night she'd saved me.

Lastly, I'd also try to come to terms with my new status in this world—my new freedom to openly share my views on how to get through this life with a solid code of ethics. Oh, and by the way, it has more to do with being the best person you can, rather than putting the fear of scripture quotes and fire and brimstone into non-believers.

I don't care if you believe. I know that sounds crazy coming from an ex-nun once deeply immersed in a convent and yards and yards of scripture. But I don't. You don't have to believe in an unseen entity if you so choose.

But I do care deeply about the world as a whole, and showing, not telling people you can live your life richly, fully, without ever stepping inside the hallowed halls of a church if you decide that's what works for you.

I want anyone who'll listen to know you can indeed have a life worth living—even as a low-level demon escaped from Hell and an ex-communicated nun who suffers from what Coop and I jokingly call demoni-phrenia.

Also known as, the occasional possession of an ex-nun cursed by a random evil spirit.

And I was determined to prove that—not only to myself, but to this spirit who had me in its greasy black clutches.

NOTE FROM DAKOTA

I do hope you enjoyed this book, I'd so appreciate it if you'd help others enjoy it too.

Recommend it. Please help other readers find this book by recommending it.

Review it. Please tell other readers why you liked this book by reviewing it at online retailers or your blog. Reader reviews help my books continue to be valued by distributors/resellers. I adore each and every reader who takes the time to write one!

If you love the book or leave a review, please email **dakota@dakotacassidy.com** so I can thank you with a personal email. Your support means more than you'll ever know! Thank you!

ABOUT THE AUTHOR

Dakota Cassidy is a USA Today bestselling author with over thirty books. She writes laugh-out-loud cozy mysteries, romantic comedy, grab-some-ice erotic romance, hot and sexy alpha males, paranormal shifters, contemporary kick-ass women, and more.

Dakota was invited by Bravo TV to be the Bravo-holic for a week, wherein she snarked the hell out of all the Bravo shows. She received a starred review from Publishers Weekly for Talk Dirty to Me, won a Romantic Times Reviewers' Choice Award for Kiss and Hell, along with many review site recommended reads and reviewer top pick awards.

Dakota lives in the gorgeous state of Oregon with her real-life hero and her dogs, and she loves hearing from readers!

OTHER BOOKS BY DAKOTA CASSIDY

Visit Dakota's website at
http://www.dakotacassidy.com for more information.

A Lemon Layne Mystery, a Contemporary Cozy Mystery Series

    1. Prawn of the Dead

    2. Play That Funky Music White Koi

Witchless In Seattle Mysteries, a Paranormal Cozy Mystery series

    1. Witch Slapped

    2. Quit Your Witchin'

    3. Dewitched

    4. The Old Witcheroo

    5. How the Witch Stole Christmas

    6. Ain't Love a Witch

    7. Good Witch Hunting

    8. Witch Way Did He Go?

Nun of Your Business Mysteries, a Paranormal Cozy Mystery series

1. Then There Were Nun
2. Hit and Nun
3. House of the Rising Nun

Wolf Mates, a Paranormal Romantic Comedy series

1. An American Werewolf In Hoboken
2. What's New, Pussycat?
3. Gotta Have Faith
4. Moves Like Jagger
5. Bad Case of Loving You

A Paris, Texas Romance, a Paranormal Romantic Comedy series

1. Witched At Birth
2. What Not to Were
3. Witch Is the New Black
4. White Witchmas

Non-Series

Whose Bride Is She Anyway?

Polanski Brothers: Home of Eternal Rest

Sexy Lips 66

Accidentally Paranormal, a Paranormal Romantic Comedy series

Interview With an Accidental—a free introductory guide to the girls of the Accidentals!

1. The Accidental Werewolf
2. Accidentally Dead
3. The Accidental Human
4. Accidentally Demonic
5. Accidentally Catty

6. Accidentally Dead, Again

7. The Accidental Genie

8. The Accidental Werewolf 2: Something About Harry

9. The Accidental Dragon

10. Accidentally Aphrodite

11. Accidentally Ever After

12. Bearly Accidental

13. How Nina Got Her Fang Back

14. The Accidental Familiar

15. Then Came Wanda

16. The Accidental Mermaid

The Hell, a Paranormal Romantic Comedy series

1. Kiss and Hell

2. My Way to Hell

The Plum Orchard, a Contemporary Romantic Comedy series

1. Talk This Way

2. Talk Dirty to Me

3. Something to Talk About

4. Talking After Midnight

The Ex-Trophy Wives, a Contemporary Romantic Comedy series

1. You Dropped a Blonde On Me

2. Burning Down the Spouse

3. Waltz This Way

Fangs of Anarchy, a Paranormal Urban Fantasy series

1. Forbidden Alpha

2. Outlaw Alpha

Made in the USA
Monee, IL
03 June 2023

35216425R00136